Mills & Boon Classics

A chance to read and collect some of the best-loved novels from Mills & Boon – the world's largest publisher of romantic fiction.

Every month, four titles by favourite Mills & Boon authors will be re-published in the *Classics* series.

A list of other titles in the *Classics* series can be found at the end of this book.

Violet Winspear

THE
LITTLE NOBODY

MILLS & BOON LIMITED
LONDON · TORONTO

First published 1971
This edition 1980

© Violet Winspear 1971

Australian copyright 1980
Philippine copyright 1980

ISBN 0 263 73242 8

Set in 11 on 13pt Baskerville

Made and printed in Great Britain by
C. Nicholls & Company Ltd
The Philips Park Press, Manchester

Mild offspring of a dark and sullen sire!
Whose modest form, so delicately fine,
   Was nursed in whirling storms,
   And cradled in the winds.

In this low vale, the promise of the year,
Serene, thou openest to the nipping gale,
   Unnoticed and alone,
   Thy tender elegance.

So virtue blooms, brought forth amid the storms
Of chill adversity; in some lone walk
   Of life she rears her head,
   Obscure and unobserved.

                Henry Kirke White.

CHAPTER ONE

THE forbidding aspect of Sea Witch made her pause by the tall iron gates and gaze with a fast-beating heart at the mullioned windows reflecting the sunset until they glowed blood-red. At either side of the gates were high walls also bathed by the westering sun and holding a fleeting warmth from the red glow which the far-down sea would soon extinguish. The walls rambled all around the house and the grounds, and above them grew the elm trees, their uneven crowns shading the peaked roofs and towers which gave the lonely house its name.

Ynis wanted, with every nerve in her body, to turn back to the village and the small inn where it was at least cosy, but her hand was impelled towards the gate by something more deeply felt than even her fear of this house that stood halfway between the moors and the sea. As she felt the cold hardness of the iron and the yielding of the gate, her body was shaken by the tremor which many people refer to as footsteps over their grave.

The gate closed behind her and the elms stood like guardsmen along the winding drive that led to the wide stone terrace flanking the mullioned façade of Sea Witch. Stone pots stood along the parapet and a kind of white flower drooped from them like tiny ballet dancers, exhausted and scented, and cold now the blaze of the sun had died away. Ynis mounted the front steps and each step towards that great oak door was as hesitant as if invisible fingers clung to her heels and tried to hold her back. She felt again like a child summoned to face a lecture from Reverend Mother. The door to her sanctum had been likewise of oak, and after a pupil had knocked it might be minutes before the entry bell was rung and a girl entered to face across the broad desk a pair of penetrating eyes.

It was said at the Convent of the Cross that Reverend Mother could see into a girl's soul, and Ynis would not have wished for such visual powers as she stood and rang the bell of Sea Witch, so many miles from the convent and that final interview with the woman who had wanted her to remain there.

'Very well, go into the world if you must,' she had said, 'but remember that you can always return to the convent if you find the life beyond its walls uncongenial, even lonely. Our door is always open to you, for a life of devotion can compensate for many things, my child.'

Ynis knew that in her kindly way Reverend Mother had been warning her that she was plain and not forward like other girls. She might find life a little harder than she bargained for . . . even as the front door of Sea Witch opened she found stern and rather contemptuous eyes looking at her. 'I should like to see Mr. Gard St. Clair.' She forced herself to sound more confident than she felt. 'The matter is rather urgent.'

With a cold flick of his eyes she knew that the man-servant registered the fact that her suède coat was thin enough to let in the cold. Her black convent shoes were so flat-heeled that she felt like a schoolgirl as a reluctant hand beckoned her into the big, stone-flagged hall – reminiscent of St. Stephen's Chapel – with a pair of massive bronze chandeliers clinging like dusty-gold tar-antulas to the age-blackened beams of the high ceiling. The web of beams added to the chilling illusion that giant spiders lurked there.

'The master is at home,' said the manservant, in a voice as chilly as the hall, 'but I cannot say for certain that he will grant you an interview. What name shall I tell him?'

Ynis told him, but saw no sign of recognition of the name on the long severe face. 'If you will wait here, Miss Raiford, I will inform the master of your request to see him. Perhaps you would care to take a seat?'

She watched him walk away with almost a guard-like precision to the end of the hall, where he disap-peared through a door concealed by shadows. She glanced at the high-backed chairs with their hard-looking seats and wandered instead to a group of framed prints on the panelled wall. As she half expected, these were as cheerless as the hall itself and must have been there as long as those monstrous chandeliers.

Was Sea Witch one of those ancient country houses with a bedchamber dedicated to a royal lady? Ynis could imagine that here in days gone by oxen had been roasted in that cavernous fireplace to feed a company of riders returning from the hunting field, flecks of horse foam on their breeches, or voluminous skirts.

Feeling cold and bunching her hands in the pockets of her coat, Ynis turned to see the manservant re-appearing from the shadows. He looked, she thought, rather like a figure from an Edwardian play, lost in time as this house was, and as the master threatened to be, with their values and their disciplines as grim as their surroundings. She felt dismally sure she had been a fool to come here, on a darkening stormy afternoon with rain in the air ... more than rain, for as the servant approached in his stately way soot fell down the great chimney to the rumble of thunder and the flicker of lightning across the armoured surfaces of the faceless knights guarding the hall.

'If you will come this way, miss, the master will spare you a few minutes of his time.'

How gracious of him, she reflected, and lightning licked across the surface of a wall mirror and she saw that she looked as thin as a cat, with huge green eyes that gleamed with the desperation of the homeless. Like a cat she had come begging for a few scraps of mercy from Gard St. Clair, and now that she had got the scent of his house she had the dismal feeling that she would go away as empty-hearted as she had ar-rived.

A door was opened and firelight leapt at her, and instinctively she wanted to run to the glow and the warmth, but was held back by the reserve drilled into her by the Sisters of the convent, and by her dislike of the man whom she saw near the fireplace, his tall figure outlined by the flames. He did not offer a hand at her entrance, and she felt a stab of resentment. He knew who she was, so why should he be polite?

The manservant closed the door and left her alone with Gard St. Clair. 'Come closer,' ordered a deep and cultured voice, and his left hand stretched to a porcelain lamp and turned the flame higher. The breath caught in her throat, for it had not been lack of courtesy, or contempt for her, which had kept him from shaking hands with her. The right sleeve of his dark smoking jacket was pinned in place, and it was empty. The right arm of this world-famous conductor of music was missing, and she had not known. And she saw more than that as she looked at him, the raven-black hair was streaked with silver, and his gaze was as cold and unwelcoming as the rain that drove down from the sky to pound the stone walls and terraces of Sea Witch.

'Doom informed me that your name is Raiford.'

'Doom . . .?' she faltered, staring with a nervous defiance at the man who had taken from her the chance of a home beyond the high walls of the convent.

'My valet.' His sardonic smile did not light up the lean dark face, with the skin drawn firmly across the well-defined cheekbones, accentuating his look of breeding, and suffering. 'I take it you are a relation of Noel Raiford?'

'I'm his – daughter.' She held herself very straight,

as if to defy him to look down on her because Noel was in prison, waiting to be tried on a forgery charge.

The intensely dark eyes ran over her and they seemed to strip the clothes from her body and to see starkly the pale covering of flesh over her fine bones. To see these not as a sensualist but as a man angrily curious about the daughter of the man who had cheated him.

'Why have you come here?' he demanded, and his voice seemed to grate with contempt. 'To beg mercy for a liar and a crook? A man, if you can call him that, who preys on the disabled in order to obtain funds so he can live a gay life himself without doing a day's honest work! Noel Raiford made a big mistake when he came to my house. I spent too many years among a lot of mixed types, and I can recognize a sycophant a mile off. I pretended to believe his tale of an invalid child in a charity hospital, and his false appeal for funds to help keep the hospital functioning. He was a fool, Miss Raiford! He should have checked on my character, not my disability, before coming hat in hand and tongue in cheek to Sea Witch! He would have found that I was never soft-hearted even if I did make music my life.'

The words died away into a silence that was curiously painful, and then sparks flew as he kicked back a log that was about to fall from the fire. Thunder rumbled again, like the deep drums far back in the orchestra, which a flick of this man's right hand had once ordered into action ... Ynis dragged her gaze from his empty sleeve, for she didn't want to pity this man who had ensured that Noel fell a victim to his own avarice.

'You knew he would alter that cheque you gave him,' she accused.

'Of course I knew!' He emphasized the words with an expressive gesture of his lean-fingered left hand, and his face in that moment made her think of Milton's satanic angel in the window of a chapel she had once seen. It was a face which at one time would have been darkly handsome, but now it was embittered, the brows drawn into a single black line above the cold eyes.

It was a frightening face to a girl who had come alone through the darkening day and the sound of storm, to be told that he had deliberately set a trap for the weak but not vicious Noel Raiford, whom she had hoped to reform by making a proper home for him, and providing the company he sought at race tracks and in bars.

Now, because of Gard St. Clair, Noel would go to prison again, and this time for several years.

'You could perhaps have talked to him,' she said. 'You're a man of authority and you might have helped him to see the error of his ways.'

'Our ways are bred in the bone,' he cut in. 'Men such as Raiford have almost a liking for prison bars, and I doubt whether a pep talk by an angel could reform them. They prey on other people like leeches and fabricate the most audacious lies in order to lay their hands on the wages of the law-abiding. He told me his daughter – you, Miss Raiford – was a chronic invalid, unable to move a hand to help herself, and in the care of nuns.'

The dark eyes dwelt on her flat-heeled shoes and thick stockings, then upon the small silver crucifix that showed against her throat in the opening of her coat. 'I don't doubt that you have been in the charge of nuns, but as you presumably walked all this way to Sea Witch from the village you are no invalid. Nor are you so helpless that you shrank from coming here to plead the case of your parent, a wastrel whom you would be wise to forget before he makes you as bad as himself.'

'You speak like a man without a scrap of pity for anyone,' she said, and she told herself she didn't care that some fearful accident had taken off his arm and robbed him of his brilliant career. She knew that he had been one of the leading orchestral conductors, with a reputation for creating great excitement with his vibrant handling of musicians and the music played by them. Sister Birdette had loved to listen to his concerts when they were broadcast on the radio, her kind and wrinkled face wearing a rapt expression as she kneaded the bread in time with the music. The little nun would have cared that he was no longer able to conduct such concerts, but Ynis felt hardened against him by his attitude towards Noel, who might go straight with a firm hand guiding him.

It meant nothing to Gard St. Clair that she would be left entirely on her own when Noel was convicted ... loneliness faced her, or a return to the sheltering walls of the convent, where the slender cypress trees con-

cealed it from the world, making it cool and enclosed.

She shivered where she stood, and abruptly he
moved away from the fire and the maimed side of him
fell into shadow.

'You chose a dreary day for your mission,' he said.
'Come closer to the fire and warm your hands.'

'I'm all right.' She thrust her hands into her pockets.
'I don't want to impose on you more than I can
help, but I did hope that you might be persuaded to
drop the forgery charge against my father. He didn't
spend the money ... you didn't give him time for
that!'

Gard St. Clair slowly raised his black eyebrows and
studied Ynis as if she were an odd specimen of moth on
the end of a sharp pin. 'Noel Raiford has passed his
infernal nerve on to you, young woman ... or is it the
surpassing innocence of the near-novitiate that makes
you speak as you do? Your father is a crook! He slipped
up and was caught, and he will pay the price, as we all
do for one sin or another. What did you expect me to
do, let him off the hook so he could go and twist some
other disabled person, perhaps with softer feelings than
I have?'

'You laid a trap for him! You guessed his game and
instead of throwing him out of your house you gave
him a cheque he could easily alter. You could have
lectured him, but you're so – so bitter with everyone—'

'My bitterness,' he grated, 'is my business. You have

wasted your time in coming here. You had better go home.'

'Thanks to you I have no home,' she retorted. 'When Noel was taken away by the police, the landlady gave me a week's notice to vacate the furnished flat. You have a big house so you can have no idea how hard it is these days to find accommodation.'

'Is this another sob story, Miss Raiford?' His face took on a scornful look. 'Are you following already in your father's footsteps?'

There are times when even the gentlest, the most humble of people are driven to such a point of desperation that they will strike out blindly in defence of themselves.

Ynis saw the ornament on a side-table, a porcelain shepherdess in a blue dress and a brimmed hat, a little dog at her slippered feet. She flew at it and with the full force of her hand sent it smashing to the rim of parquet beyond the carpet. It broke into many small pieces, and she didn't care; she was glad that it had been pretty and valuable, and was now as broken as her hopes of making a new life for Noel and herself.

She looked defiantly at Gard St. Clair, the green of her eyes as stormy as the waters that crashed so high over the rocks of Barbizon, this coastal village in Cornwall, to which she had come from the city to see a man who had no mercy in him.

'You will pick up every piece,' he said in a cold voice. 'I have a cat who comes in here to play and I shouldn't want her to injure a paw on all that shattered

16

porcelain. Be quick about it, and then please leave my house.'

If he had stormed at her about the value of the object, she might not have felt a sudden rush of guilt and regret. She knelt, and as she picked up the scraps of blue skirt, tiny broken feet in pink slippers, and the ear of the dog, the miserable tears rushed into her eyes and she was so blinded by them that she couldn't see clearly. Pain stabbed her hand and a trickle of crimson ran down her thumb. She lifted the thumb and sucked it, and at the same time she heard the impatient ringing of the bell beside the icy figure of Gard St. Clair.

Within a matter of minutes the door opened and the dour manservant entered. 'Doom, there has been a slight accident. Will you dispose of those remains, and fetch sticking plaster for the young woman's hand.'

Doom stood staring at the girl on her knees, with a little mound of shattered porcelain in front of her. She raised to St. Clair a white, more forlorn than frightened face. She was almost at that stage of misery when violence would have come as a relief. This cold, harsh acceptance of her childish fury was hard to endure. It made of her a hasty little vixen, and confirmed his accusation . . . yet though she always spoke of Noel Raiford as her father, she had been two years old when her mother had married him. Gina had been a model, and a Welsh artist was the real father of Ynis, whose name meant 'island' in the Celtic language. Her mother had vanished out of her life when she was five, and Noel had taken her to the convent and left her there in the good care of the Sisters. Once or twice a year he had paid her a visit, and she had a certain affection for him, that of a young girl who had no other known relative to care much about her.

Noel had seemed pleased when she had said she was leaving the convent in order to make a proper home for him . . . now all she could do was return to the Sisters and perhaps become one of them. Even if she found a job, she had nowhere to stay. No friend who could give her a bed for a while. No money to pay for a room in a lodging house.

With foolish gallantry, the wild hope that this man at Sea Witch might relent, she had spent almost her last pound on the train fare and a room for the night at the Ragged Priest Inn down in the village.

She was holding her handkerchief around her thumb and avoiding the gaze of Gard St. Clair when the manservant returned with the adhesive tape. He handed her a strip and she applied it to the cut. She felt miserable and it would have been so easy to break down and cry, but tears, she had been taught, were a wasteful luxury if spent on oneself. Tilting her chin, she told St. Clair that she was ready to leave.

'I apologize for wasting your time,' she said, and regarded him with eyes that no longer pleaded in vain. She felt achingly as if she had thrown herself against a stone wall, so adamant was this man who stood so un-moving beside the fireplace.

'And what about the porcelain girl?' he asked. 'It was valuable and you deliberately smashed it. I am entitled to demand payment.'

'I have no money,' she said tonelessly. 'You had better have me charged along with Noel.'

'That would really set you on the road to ruin, wouldn't it?' His look was sardonic, and then he made a slight movement and she quickly retreated from him before she realized that he had taken a flat gold case from his pocket and flipped it open. He stood it on the mantelpiece and took from it a cheroot. 'Doom! I think you had better show Miss Raiford to the front door.'

'Yes, sir.' But as he spoke the manservant seemed to hesitate for a moment, and to glance at the windows, across which heavy curtains were drawn. Then he glanced at Ynis and she preceded him from the room, feeling the chill of the hall as she stepped beyond the bounds of the log fire. It seemed an endless walk to the front door and there she paused to push her coat collar up about her face as Doom opened the great slab of oak and iron. The wind blew in at her and it was filled with rain. The rain stung her with its coldness as she stepped out of the unwelcoming house into the cheerless night.

The cold wind struck through the thinness of her coat, and the cut on her hand stung as she pressed the collar close to her face. 'Good night,' she said to Doom.

'Miss – let me fetch you an umbrella!'

The offer so surprised her with its unexpected concern that when she turned to look at him, and the porch-light showed the immensity of her eyes against the thin, pale angularity of her face, she looked like an under-fed cat, to whom few people had been indulgent.

'Thank you,' she said, 'but the wind would probably blow it inside out.'

'You have a long walk, miss, to the village.'

'I'm a quick walker.' She started off down the long drive, guarded by its elms that now had a curious witch-look as the wind blew their crowns. The trees half sheltered her until she reached the road, which was open to the elements from the moors and the sea. Ynis knew that if she just kept walking she would eventually come in sight of the cottage lights of the village that wended its way past boat sheds and lumber yards, until she reached the Ragged Priest that was quite close to the railway station.

She plunged on through the windswept night and she didn't know herself if it was rain or tears on her face. She had never felt so alone, or so defeated. She had been warned that the world was large, and hearts not always charitable ... but she had never dreamed that a man could be so devoid of charity as the man she had just left, smoking alone in his warm and well-furnished room, as unmoved by her appeal as if he were made of stone.

How dark this road was, so that every few yards she stumbled against the grass verge, or was half blown over by a fiercer gust of wind. She longed for a glimpse of the village lights and for a hot cup of tea at the inn. She was resolved not to think about tomorrow until it came, or the narrowing down of her horizon to one of duty and dedication, and the wearing of the plain habit that would no doubt suit her. She mustn't think of the pictures in that magazine left on the train, of girls in silk dresses being escorted to restaurants and theatres by young men in dinner suits ... she must quench the memory of her gay young mother who had run out on her duties.

Oh, this wind, if only it would change its direction and not blow the rain in her face all the time. The dampness had seeped through her coat, and her hair was blown about her temples like whips. Her hands were chilled, and she had the forlorn feeling that she was the only human creature out on such a night. Everyone else was close to a warm fire, safe and secure in congenial company.

How she hated Gard St. Clair! He hadn't really listened to her, or been moved by a word she had said. The only emotion he had shown had been that of the icy recluse determined to have his revenge against every law-breaker who came within reach of his cold brain and his colder heart. She felt sure he had enjoyed treating her like a little alley cat ... and she wasn't sorry, not a bit sorry that she had smashed his porcelain lady ... the only sort he could love!

These were the thoughts predominant in her mind as she rounded a bend in the road and was abruptly blinded by the oncoming headlamps of a fast-moving car. She threw up her arms as the vehicle rushed out of the rain-swept night and she was like a supplicant again, begging mercy of a force that could not or would not grant it. She was hit and she was down, and everything was going so rapidly dark that she knew she must be dying. She gave a cry and gave in to the darkness, and the last thing she felt was her face striking with pain against the cold wet verge to which she had been flung by the unfaltering speed of the car that sped on and didn't stop.

Like a hare she had been run down, and left, while the rain fell . . . and fell.

CHAPTER TWO

THERE was a cold sound of rain beating against the windows, the sighing of the wind in the trees, and the shimmer of long silk curtains in the firelight. She seemed to drift out of a frightening dream to find herself quite safe, snug in a huge warm bed, with the softness of large pillows beneath her head. With wondering, drowsy eyes she gazed at the tiger-head rug that lay snarling in front of the fire.

Even as she absorbed the beauty and comfort of the room, she had a vague recollection of a harder bed than this one, of a wooden floor without rugs, and narrow windows covered by thick white netting. But the memory was so intangible that it was surely part of the strange dream from which she had just woken.

A smile touched her lips. She must often have lain on the striped pelt with the fierce, handsome head attached, no doubt reading one of the books that reposed in the cabinet with the curly Chinese carving. Her gaze turned drowsily to the lamp that burned softly at her bedside; it was shaded to match the curtains and there was a peacock painted on the china stand. Its prettiness gave her a little shock of pleasure. From the look of this room there could never have been a moment when she had not lived among pretty things. Those ballerina pictures on the wall were so charming that the girls in them seemed about to dance out of the frames to perform a ballet for her.

Ynis sighed with sleepy pleasure ... and then she tensed as the rain rattled harder against the curtained windows. How awful not to be protected and warm as she was but out in the wind and the wet, with no home like this to go to. She snuggled down in her bed and felt so thankful that she was here and not wandering homeless in the night. She fell asleep and this time the dream did not return to make her restless.

With the arrival of morning came a woman in a starched cap and a crisp blue uniform, so cheerful and real as she pulled back the curtains and let the morning sunlight into the room. 'And how's my patient?' she asked.

Her patient studied her with a look of surprise. 'I've been ill!'

Now in the morning light she gazed around the room and saw that everything was the same as it had been last night ... except that the rain had stopped beating against the windows.

The nurse smiled and helped her to sit up, banking the pillows behind her thin shoulders. 'There, does that feel better?' The woman spoke in a voice with a pleasant burr to it. 'Are you going to enjoy your breakfast today, dearie? Yesterday you weren't too willing and I had to coax you, but today your eyes are brighter. You seem much more aware of yourself.'

'Yes, I do feel better.' The big green eyes stared at the nurse. 'What has been the matter with me? How long have I been ill?'

'You were knocked down by a hit-and-run car, dearie. Left there by the roadside to get your death of cold in the rain – if Mr. Doom hadn't found you.'

'Doom?' Ynis spoke the name with a slight catch of her breath, as if she faintly recalled it. 'I seem to know – to have heard it before.'

'Now don't force yourself to remember,' said the nurse. 'Everything will come back to you in time, for it was a nasty crack on the head you took and you've been concussed for almost three weeks. Been like a child, you have.'

'A child?' The green eyes, the only features that held any colour in the fragile face, stared at the hands that gripped the silk coverlet. The fingernails of each hand were cut short and unpolished. The right hand was bare and still showed the marks of a graze. But on the left hand there was a ring and she studied it with wonderment. It was a gold band most beautifully set with a moon sapphire slightly raised upon a bed of tiny pearls. To even say the ring was exquisite was not to describe it, and she felt her heart beat fast with the realization that it was firmly placed upon the third finger of her left hand.

She glanced up at the nurse, and was suddenly driven by a curiosity almost primeval to ask for a hand mirror. 'I – I can't seem to remember what I look like. Isn't it absurd?'

With an indulgent look on her face the nurse went to the dressing-table and returned with a silver-backed mirror, which she held so the green eyes could study the face in which they were set slightly aslant beneath the flyaway eyebrows.

'How thin my face is! I – I couldn't be called pretty, could I!'

'Think of all you've been through, dearie.' The nurse spoke in a bracing voice. 'Besides, what do looks matter? You have a fiancé, haven't you? Love and beauty are in the eyes of the beholder, and now your eyes are much brighter I can see what a vivid green they are. Funny though—' The nurse paused and considered the girl in the big bed, with her eyes fixed again on the lovely ring that dominated her left hand.

The green eyes lifted to the face of the nurse. 'What is funny – that some man should fancy a piece of skin and bone like me?'

The nurse gave a laugh. 'Ah yes, you're getting better! When a patient starts to talk back, then we know that she's really on the mend. No, I was just thinking that with your eyes a man should choose a gem of the same colour, instead of that deep blue. It's lovely, of course, but men don't always show a lot of imagination – though I must say *he* looks a deep one.'

'Tell me what he's like—' The small teeth bit down on the lips that were pale with a sensitive shape to them. 'It's really odd not being able to remember the simplest things, such as my own name, and the face of my – fiancé. Is he nice?'

It was the turn of the nurse to bite her lip. 'He's a

26

masterful man, I'll say that for him, for all that he—'

'Yes, go on!' Ynis strained forward in the bed, eager for details to fill in those disturbing blanks in her mind. 'I – I'm like the sleeping princess who has just woken up after a long time. Is he tall, and fair, and does he love to ride a horse? Somehow I have the feeling that I could only marry the outdoor type who always smells of the wind and the sea.'

'Fair he isn't.' The nurse gave a rather forced laugh. 'You'll be seeing him soon enough, and right now I'm off to fetch your breakfast tray. Do you fancy eggs with toast, and fruit to follow?'

'How soon shall I see him – and, Nurse, what is his name?' It was a cry from the heart, an appeal not to be ignored. The nurse stood with a hand gripping the knob of the bedroom door, and then she turned to face the youthful figure in the king-sized bed.

'He's Gard St. Clair, a gentleman of means, and clever as the dev—' She broke off and bustled away, leaving in the air the word she had made significant by breaking it in half.

St. Clair's fiancée sat against her pillows and repeated to herself the name of the man to whom she was en-gaged. It was a name suggestive of ownership, of some-one who kept an eagle eye on what was his. She fingered the sapphire that burned with a deep blue flame, a ring that proclaimed that it had been given with love, and suddenly she was rather afraid of this man who had a claim upon her, whom she could not remember. A man of means, and clever as the devil!

Her hand shook slightly as she picked up the mirror which the nurse had left on the bedside table, and once again she took a long, objective look at her own face. Was this the kind of face a man of means might love? Was this almost boyishly slim body of hers capable of arousing passion in a strong-willed man?

As yet her own name eluded her, but she had not forgotten the basic facts of life even if she could not remember if she had a family, or was alone in the world but for this fiancé who seemed to have an odd effect upon her nurse. Charming men, nice men, didn't make women evasive, or inclined to use the word 'devil' in reference to them.

The mirror sank face down on the coverlet of thick pearly silk, and now in daylight the green eyes took a more intent look at the bedroom, with its pearly satin boudoir chairs, and tiger-headed pelt upon the deep creamy carpet that covered all the floor. Cascades of silk and net hung at the long windows, beyond which she could hear the crying of birds . . . seabirds!

So wherever she was, she was close to the sea! And the house was big, if this room and those windows were anything to go by. Whose house was it? The blue ring weighted her hand to the bed and gave her the answer.

The door opened and the nurse returned with a tray on which stood things of silver and delicate china. Little legs unfolded so the tray could be placed firmly across the lap of the patient. 'There you are, dearie. The toast is all nice and hot and wrapped in a napkin.

The eggs are fresh laid this morning—'

'Nurse?'

'Yes, dearie? Do you want to use the bathroom before you start on your breakfast?'

'No – but do tell me where I am! Is this my home? A private clinic – or the house of Gard St. Clair?'

'Bless you, this is Sea Witch, one of the oldest and finest houses in this part of Cornwall. Of course it's Mr. St. Clair's house. It was his manservant who found you . . . for a week you were in hospital, and then it was arranged that the ambulance bring you to Sea Witch, and I came along to look after you.' The nurse poured coffee from the silver pot into the cup. 'Now drink up and eat and don't let all this good food grow cold.'

'Wasn't there anywhere else I could go?' She had shivered at the name of the house, as if for her it was not a happy name.

'Why should you want to, dearie? When Mr. St. Clair has done his best for you, and paid to have me here. He thought it would be nicer for you than being in hospital, and you must admit that your room is luxury itself.' As the nurse spoke she draped a bed-jacket of peach-coloured quilted silk about the young pale shoulders. 'There, now enjoy your breakfast and do stop worrying. I know it must bewilder you, not being able to recall the names and faces of people close to you, but all of a sudden, just like the shutter of a camera, something will click in your mind and you'll be your old self again. Physically you're heaps better – is your egg just right?'

'Fine, thank you.' She ate egg and toast, and drank her coffee, and then she had to say the thing that sounded so funny, even to herself. 'I don't even know my own name, but I feel sure it must be Jane. Plain Jane!'

The nurse laughed, half-way to a door in an alcove of the large room. 'You are a bit of a card, dearie. Here you are, surrounded by lovely things provided by the man you're going to marry, and you talk about yourself like that. As a matter of fact you have a very unusual name. I'd never heard it before I came here to nurse you—'

'I'd like to hear my blessed name!' The green eyes were beseeching. 'And don't disappear through any more doors before telling me.'

'Your name is Ynis – now isn't that unusual? I asked Mr. Doom about it, and he said it might be Welsh. Ynis Raiford, that's what you're called, and now I'll go and run you a bath, and put in lots of those scented crystals so you'll be sweet for Mr. St. Clair when he comes to see you.'

'He's coming – to my room?' A spoon clattered into the saucer of the coffee cup.

'Bless you, yes. I saw him when I went for your tray and I told him how perky you were today. He said he'd be along in about two hours, after he's got off his morning mail and seen his estate manager.'

'Oh, lord!' The very thought of seeing him made Ynis feel unbearably edgy ... this was the man she must love, if she was wearing his ring, yet he would come to her a stranger, for try as she might she couldn't remember a detail of her engagement to him; she couldn't recall how it felt to be kissed, and so wanted that a man wished to marry her. She longed to ask for a detailed description of him, but already the nurse was in the bathroom and the sound of rushing water could be heard. Ynis stared at the peach on her plate, big and velvety smooth to the touch. She was being so cared for, so pampered, that Gard St. Clair must care for her very much . . . lord, how awful it was, not to be able to remember him!

'Now eat that peach,' said the nurse, bustling back into the room and taking a brisk look at the tray. 'It was grown in the conservatory and looks delicious.'

'I'm not hungry any more – you eat it.' Ynis handed the tray to the nurse, who after making clucking noises with her tongue made short and greedy work of the juicy peach. 'Better than wasting it, but you must eat, dearie, if you're going to get strong and well. You won't remember all those things you've forgotten until you're really well, you know. Now shall we pop into the bathroom and have a splash about in that pink and black tub fit for a film star?'

'Yes – but let me try and walk on my own.' Ynis put back the covers and swung her legs to the floor. When she stood up she swayed slightly from weakness, but after a few seconds she was able to make her way across the soft carpet to the bathroom, but once they were in there the nurse insisted on helping her into the warm and scented water. The tub was immense, with silver faucets in the shape of swan heads. There was an attached shower, a headrest, and handles for pulling herself in and out of the bath.

Even as she luxuriated in the warm and aromatic water there swept over her again that vagrant feeling that she had once known surroundings as spartan as these were splendid. What was the truth about her? Was she a working girl who through some quirk of destiny had met the owner of all this and made him love her?

It was strange that if she had loved, and been loved, so stirring an experience had left no deep impression on her senses. Even if one forgot the names of people, and even their features, the heart retained the glow which had been lighted there. A warm expectation should be hers, not this chilly apprehension when she thought of her imminent meeting with Gard St. Clair.

She studied her bare-shouldered reflection in the mirrored wall . . . it was possible that she was marrying this man for his money, yet she didn't look much of a gold-digger. Her brown hair looked as if it had been cut short at one time and was now growing a trifle unevenly, framing a face that seemed innocent enough. It didn't look the type of face to deceive a man . . . those large, rather slanting eyes held uncertainty rather than the audacity of a girl who had set out to marry money.

The moon sapphire glowed on her hand as she slowly raised it to her throat and felt the pulse that beat quickly there. Perhaps when she saw him she would feel entirely at her ease. Perhaps it was only her amnesia which made her feel this sense of fear.

She was out of the water and towelling herself when the nurse returned with a fresh nightdress and a robe over her arm.

'I want to get properly dressed,' Ynis told her. 'I – I don't want to be in bed when he comes to my room.'

'He won't mind.' The nurse gave her a curious look, with a touch of coyness in it. 'All right, I won't argue with you, but you must stay in your room and sit in the armchair. You still aren't fit enough to roam about the house.'

'Just so long as I'm dressed.' Ynis took the silk robe and put it on. 'Shall we take a look in the clothes closet?'

It was a white louvred one that ran the length of the bedroom, and Ynis gasped to see it filled with clothes for every occasion, also shoes and a nest of drawers filled with delicate, expensive lingerie in shades of pale coffee and palest green. In another compartment there were nylons, bags and gloves, and a selection of beautiful silk scarves. And over all hung a delicate wisp of perfume ... a flower scent with the faintest hint of musk.

'Wow!' Ynis could not help herself from giving voice to the expression. 'Are all these mine?'

'They're your size, dearie,' said the nurse, speaking indulgently but looking faintly envious. 'Now which dress are you going to wear – no, you can't wear that!'

Ynis smiled, for she was fingering the full lace skirt of a pale-pink ball dress, so incredibly pretty that it had to be a couture creation; a model gown which had surely never been worn. She ran her hand along the rack of dresses and it struck her that none of them had ever been worn; they were all brand new, with silk labels in them, and with filmy-silk linings to the blouses and skirts; an exquisite tailored look to the slacks, with their pencil-slim line.

No working girl would possess such clothes ... unless ... Ynis bit her lip and felt for a moment as if her body were on fire. Had she sold herself already for the pot of gold?

'These must be your trousseau.' The nurse took a golden wool dress off its hanger. 'Now this is nice, modom. How about wearing this for your first morning out of bed? Look, shoes to match, and nylons like cobwebs. You're the lucky one, you are, for all that you can't remember that dark man of yours.'

'Is he dark?' Ynis spoke almost in a whisper, and that feeling of heat gave way to one of shivery fear again.

'Dark as the dev – well, he's Cornish, and it's traditional for the men of these parts to be "black-browed", as we say.'

Ynis was silent a moment, then she turned away from the array of lovely clothes for all occasions, even balls, and she couldn't remember ever having been to a ball. 'Yes, that dress will do. Let's hurry or he'll be here before I'm ready.'

'Dearie, have you gone all shy of him?' laughed the nurse. 'He's seen you in your bed more than once – never spared a day without coming to take a look at you to see how you were getting along.'

'Well,' said Ynis, 'it will be quite a surprise for him to see me out of bed and dressed. I have the feeling that men are not enamoured of sick people – and you said he was clever, and clever people are sometimes impatient.'

'That blow on the head hasn't knocked out your wits, anyway. Mmm, I do like this dress, but you have lost some weight! See how closely the belt cinches in? You've almost one of those hand-span waists, dearie.'

Ynis frowned slightly and wished the woman would call her anything but 'dearie'. She was kind, of course, but it would be a relief to be rid of such constant attention. 'I really can manage to put on my own nylons,' she sighed. 'Look, why don't you run along and have a coffee break?'

'Getting fed up with me?' The nurse looked knowing. 'It's always the first sign that a nurse had better start packing her bag.'

'It isn't that I'm ungrateful,' Ynis said, contritely. 'But I don't think I'm used to being fussed over. It feels – alien to me. Do you happen to know anything about me, apart from the fact that I was knocked down by a car, and I'm engaged to Gard St. Clair? It might help my memory to be told a few facts of my life.'

'Oh, I think you should leave it to *him* to tell you

35

the relevancies, dearie. All I know is that you're his girl, and if a man was willing to make me the mistress of a house as big as this one I wouldn't bother myself asking too many questions. Men enjoy mysteries—'

'Do you think I'm a mystery?' Ynis broke in. 'Is that how I strike you?'

'Well, I suppose one would expect a man of means to marry a girl of his own class, but people these days are a bit more democratic, and perhaps in the circumstances—' The nurse paused in her brushing of her patient's hair and she stared into the dressing table mirror at the reflected face of Ynis. A fine-boned face, with shadows under the high cheekbones, and almost a transparency to the eyelids so that the green of her eyes seemed to reflect a greenish shadow, the sort that another girl might paint there. It was a strange, disturbing face, not pretty to the average onlooker, but an artist might have seen something there to intrigue him.

'Now you are being mysterious, Nurse,' she said. 'What set of circumstances could make it right for a man of property to want a girl like me? I'm not pretty, and as far as I know I'm not a gifted person, or a fascinating actress . . . or am I?' She stared at her own face in the mirror . . . had there been a time, before a car had run into her and erased her memory, when she had played a part and pretended love for this man whom she sensed from the nurse's manner to be a difficult and demanding person?

Was it even possible that she had really loved him

36

... this stranger whose expensive ring adorned her hand, and looked so oddly as if it belonged upon a smooth and manicured hand, with almond-shaped fingernails, uncut and carefully polished?

'I'm not saying another word.' The nurse gave a rather nervous laugh, and with determination she led Ynis to a deep armchair by the long french windows and made her sit down and relax. She placed a cushion behind her shoulders and gave her thin cheek a light pat. 'Now you stay there and look at the garden and don't make another move. You don't want to have me fired outright by "the master" as Mr. Doom calls him, now do you?'

Ynis smiled faintly and shook her head. 'You're kind to me and I really do appreciate it – why, I never realized this room was on the ground floor!' She gazed across the terrace, to the lawns and the big sprawling beds of azaleas, dark flame in the cool sunlight, against the close-cut grass. 'How odd – one always imagines that bedrooms are above the stairs – or has this room been converted for my use, while I've been concussed and adrift from reality? I – I can't even remember being brought here!'

'That's how it is with concussion,' the nurse said soothingly. 'All this wing of Sea Witch is converted and modern, and very nice too. The west wing is older and not much used, apart from the study, where Mr. St. Clair does a lot of his work.' She paused and seemed to listen, and then she made for the door. 'I'm off to have that cup of coffee and a doughnut. It's almost time for your fiancé to call on you. 'Bye now!'

The door closed behind her plump figure and Ynis was left alone, to listen to the birds calling to each other as they flew among the chimneys of Sea Witch, flying in from the ocean with the freedom and grace of winged souls. And as she listened she caught another sound, that of firm footfalls coming along the stone paving of the terrace that was framed by the long windows of her room, with its ornamental balustrade and its pots that spilled a ferny plant, white-flowered, against the dark grey stonework.

She leaned forward in her chair and her heart beat quickly, and then seemed to turn over in her breast as a tall man came into view. Ynis stared through the glass at him, and he paused and gazed back at her, intently, without a shadow of a smile on his dark face. Then he opened the french doors and stepped into her room, closing them behind him with his left hand.

'Good morning, Ynis. I was informed that you were feeling a lot better today.' He spoke in a deep voice that somehow matched his person, in a tone that was quite impersonal, but even as the hope leapt in her that he was not Gard St. Clair, he added: 'I realize that you are still suffering from amnesia and that I must seem a stranger to you.' His eyes searched her face, taking in the pallor that intensified the jade colour of her eyes. 'Do I frighten you? Have you forgotten entirely that I was like this, unable to take you in my arms?'

She tried to control the tremor that shook her, and to keep her eyes from dwelling with a shocked look

38

upon that empty right sleeve, pinned flatly against his side. There was about him such a dark, strong grace of body that it seemed extra awful that his body should be mutilated in any way.

'You don't remember me, eh?'

It was easier to let him believe that her mind was still a complete blank, but she knew, as he stood there outlined by the morning light streaming through the windows, that in some corner of her hazy mind his image was indelibly printed. Every nerve in her body responded to his image . . . what was missing was the remotest feeling of love, or longing. What she felt, as he came towards her, was a sense of fear that made her want to leap to her feet and dash away from him. He seemed, as he stood looking down at her, to throw a shadow over the day which had started so hopefully.

CHAPTER THREE

'Sit back and relax,' he ordered. 'You still look as if a breath of wind might blow you over. Did you eat a good breakfast?'

'Yes, thank you.' She knew she ought to try and smile at him, to show a glimmer of gratitude for his concern over her, but her facial muscles wouldn't obey her and all she could do was sit there, like a nervous adolescent, her hands clasped together as if she prayed that it wasn't really true she was bound to marry this man. It wasn't his disability from which she shrank; it was the remote darkness of his eyes which filled her with a lonely sort of terror. They might have been fine eyes, had they ever smiled, but she had the feeling he had not really smiled for a long time.

'Though at present I seem a stranger to you, you must try and call me Gard,' he said firmly. 'What will people think if you remain so formal with the man you are going to marry?'

To hear him put it into words stabbed her into a quick retort. 'Do you care what people think?' she asked. 'You don't strike me that way.'

One of the thick black brows that shaded his eyes slowly arched and increased his sardonic look. 'You seem to know me even though you can't quite remember me. No, I don't care at all if people dislike me, and treat me as if I am alien instead of merely disabled. But I should prefer to be thought a desirable future husband instead of a monster – if you don't mind.'

'I – I don't regard you as a monster,' she protested. 'If I seem distant it's because this – this fog over my mind makes me that way. I am like a book with a chapter torn out. I don't know whom I have loved, and whom I have disliked.'

'It must be a very bewildering feeling, Ynis.'

She nodded, and it struck her that in his sardonic way he was being sympathetic. There was no love in his gaze, not a hint of compassion, but there was a magnetic assurance that made him seem more forceful than men who had the full use of their physiques. She felt suddenly glad that he was not her enemy.

'Do you find this room restful?' He glanced around him, and when his gaze rested upon the bed she was made aware of the number of times he had seen her slim and lost in it, pleasantly adrift in a world of her own which had not included him . . . as this awakening must include him. He had seen to it that she had every comfort, so how could she ask him to let her go?

'It's a very beautiful room,' she said politely. 'My nurse tells me that I am in the modernized wing of Sea Witch.'

'Yes.' He sat down on the foot of the chaise-longue patterned with silky *fleurs de lotus*, and looked darkly forbidding against the silk. 'We shall be living here in the south wing when we are married. You don't remember yet that I had the redecorating done as a sort of wedding gift, because the west wing is a trifle old and grim for a brand new bride. I always felt these terrace rooms were wasted as libraries, reception and flower rooms. Now we have a complete suite to ourselves, connected by the terrace which catches most of the sunlight and is not exposed to the sea wind like the west side. Of course the view is not quite so dramatic, but modern young women prefer comfort to scenery.'

'Do they?' She looked at him gravely for each thing he said seemed to underline how much she had forgotten, and how much she must remember before she and Gard St. Clair could really talk together as two people who had chosen to become man and wife. Was he hinting, when he spoke of what modern girls liked, that her motive was a mercenary one and no secret as far as he was concerned? She quickly lowered her lashes so she didn't have to look at his face, and the feeling was a disconcerting one that he knew her so much better than she knew herself. She felt that he played with her, as if she were a moth on a pin, whose flutterings he rather enjoyed.

'I seem to have forgotten a number of things,' she said, and she knew there was a defensive note in her voice. 'I'm such a stranger to myself that I don't know my own age, or where I come from. I asked the nurse, but she thought it better that I ask you. Will you oblige?'

'I'd like to, Ynis, but I can't be definite about your age or even your abode before you came to me.'

'What do you mean?' Her lashes lifted and her eyes

showed him some of the antagonism which his strange, mocking personality aroused in her. 'Why can't you be straight with me instead of intimating all the time that I am some sort of a – a *femme fatale*?'

'You?' His eyes quizzed her mockingly, for even the expensive dress she wore couldn't hide her lack of poise, which was, presumably, an attribute of the fatal charmer. She felt the colour burn high on her cheekbones, for he made no pretence of caring for her in a personal sense. What in heaven's name held them together? What made two people become engaged when they obviously had nothing in common?

'You aren't very old,' he said. 'Still young enough to blush.'

'Then you must tell me who you are.' She was pressing her hands so tightly together that his ring was hurting her bones. 'We seem an oddly assorted couple . . . you are a man of property and I seem to be a little nobody.'

'Both facts are indisputable,' he agreed, 'but I do assure you that it isn't the first time in the annals of romantic history that a "little nobody" has married rather well . . . in a financial sense, of course.' He glanced sideways at his empty sleeve. 'I hope this doesn't put you off? I could tell when I stepped through those doors that you had entirely forgotten that I was maimed.'

She flinched at the word, but when his eyelids narrowed she knew at once that he thought she flinched from him. 'I'm sorry about your arm and I don't find it

43

in the least unsightly.'

'Which is just as well, Ynis, as you will be living with me.' He paused a moment, significantly. 'And what would you like to know about me, apart from the fact that I own Sea Witch and its surrounding acres, and have Cornish-Breton blood in my veins? There used to be a saying in the old days that a man of that lineage was bound to be a pirate.'

'In the old days?' she murmured, and her gaze flashed over the dark contours of his face, meaningly. She saw his upper lip twitch, perhaps with a ghost of a smile.

'I was a conductor of music,' he said explicitly. 'Now I am what is politely termed a "gentleman farmer", meaning that I keep the books while others reap and sow for me. Mainly the unglamorous potato. I also have some cattle, and the conservatories produce quite a good crop of tomatoes and fruit. Hardly a pirate, you see.'

'How long since—?' Her left hand clenched her right one, and it was a gesture which spoke more eloquently than words.

'Five years,' he said, completely understanding her. 'I don't wish to discuss that aspect of my life, so we'll drop the subject now and for good. Do you understand? Even when you become my wife I don't want you to assume that it then becomes a subject for discussion. It happened before we ever met. The man I then was, and the man I now am, are two totally different people, with separate aims in life.'

'Meaning,' she said quietly, 'that I should have had no place in your – previous life?'

He shrugged and looked about him, with signs of restlessness. 'I wish to smoke and hardly think it suitable to do so in your bedroom. Do you think you feel fit enough to walk with me to the lounge? It's only a few doors along the terrace.'

When she nodded he rose to his feet and went to the clothes cupboard. He opened it and took from it a creamy lambswool coat, which he swung about her shoulders before they stepped out on to the terrace. 'It won't hurt you to get a breath of sea air, but I don't want you to catch cold. After all, our wedding is all arranged. When I was told this morning that you were feeling so much better, I telephoned the Vicar—'

'But I can't marry a stranger!' Even as the words came from her heart itself, she reached out to clutch at the arm that wasn't there. Instead she touched his empty sleeve, gripped it a moment to steady herself, and then let go as if the material could burn her.

'We aren't strangers, Ynis,' he said, looking down at her with cool, almost calculating eyes. 'I do assure you that we know each other very well.'

'Do we – love each other?' she asked, and met his eyes, there by the terrace parapet, swathed in the fur that felt so strange about her thin body. Was it memory, or was it instinct, that assured her she had never worn this coat before? Though it fitted her as if made for her, it felt as if it must surely belong to some-

45

one more lovely than she, more worldly ... and loved.

'Many marriages are made on this earth,' he rejoined. 'They are not always motivated by undying love. You wear my ring, Ynis. I intend that you should abide by the meaning of it. Come, you wouldn't jilt me, would you?'

'How would that be possible?' she asked. 'When you intend to make me abide by a promise I can't even remember making.' She breathed the cool and tangy air blowing up the slope of the lawns, as if she might clear that bewildering mist from her mind. 'I can smell the sea – it's very invigorating.'

'Yes, this is a rather spellbinding part of the Cornish coast, with the mingled attractions of ocean and moorland. Sea Witch is isolated, of course, but you were never a girl for the high life.'

'Wasn't I?' She had to smile a little, for it sounded strange to have to be told her own likes and dislikes. 'I noticed that I speak differently from my nurse, which must mean that I am not a country girl.'

'You come from London.' He ushered her in through the french doors of the lounge, but she had eyes only for him.

'You told me you weren't sure of my background!'

'London is a big place, Ynis.' He took the fur coat from her shoulders and laid it across the back of a silk Empire settee. 'We never got around to discussing exactly where you were born, but I do know that part of your life was spent in a convent school.'

'The charity sort?' She stood staring at the classic marbled fireplace and the exquisite painting above the mantel of a Regency child sitting in a windowseat with a small dog in her lap. Her eyes left the painting to take in the elegance of the room, the golden panelling of the walls, the crystal wall-lights, the sofa chairs covered with a detailed silk, the turquoise carpet, and the marquetry cabinets and matching card-table. It was a room in which each piece had been chosen with the care and taste of a man of the world. It revealed his love of beauty and grace . . . yet catching sight of herself in one of the scrolled mirrors, Ynis was bewildered anew that he chose a little nobody like herself for his future wife.

She turned to look at him, as if to read in his unreadable face the reason for choosing her when he must know women who would add grace to this room. 'Sit down,' he said. 'You can have some tea while I smoke one of my infernal cheroots. I can't seem to do without them, so you will have to get used to the tang of them.' He pressed a wall bell as he spoke, then he opened a silver box that stood on the mantelpiece, took from it a cheroot and placed it between his lips. He picked up the lighter, spun the wheel and put the flame to the tip of the dark cheroot. There was no clumsiness at all in the way he used his left hand, Ynis noticed, but he had been a conductor of music and it must have been terrible for him to lose that right arm. To possess no longer the agility of the right wrist, and the supple play of the baton in the hand and fingers extending from that wrist. His refusal to talk about the accident could only mean that five years had not softened the blow.

A maid in a uniform of pale tan, with a white starched collar and cap, came in answer to the service bell. He ordered a pot of tea on a tray and oven-scones with jam. She bobbed and closed the door behind her, and it struck Ynis that in an isolated house such as Sea Witch the old customs and courtesies would be retained. A certain grace of living would be demanded by the man who stood dark and well-dressed by the marble fireplace, where an electric fire glowed with the realistic look of logs in flames.

'You are looking about you,' he drawled, 'as if you feel like a fish hooked out of its small pond of water.'

'It must be my convent upbringing which makes me gasp and look pop-eyed at the splendour of your big sea house.' She looked at him and felt annoyed by his sardonic air of knowing the world as she could never know it . . . driven into words that were almost impudent and surely alien to her nature. 'What on earth have we in common? Even your ring doesn't match my eyes, which in case you haven't noticed are green.'

He gazed directly into her eyes, and then drew deeply on his cheroot and allowed the smoke to drift from the chiselled arch of his nostrils. 'Are you quibbling about receiving a sapphire instead of a jade to match those witch's eyes of yours? That ring is worth a devil of a lot of money.'

'I'd hate to think I was mercenary,' she retorted, and

48

the skin over her cheekbones tingled, and that tingling feeling seemed to spread over her body. 'I – I don't feel like a gold-digger, and I'm certain I don't look like one.'

'How do you imagine a gold-digger looks?' His eyes were mocking as he regarded her through his cheroot smoke. 'It isn't always easy to tell the genuine from the false. The face can be the most deceptive of masks. A voice can lead the devil on. Are you thinking it takes beauty and a seductive shape?'

'If a man like yourself is to be led on,' she said, and her flash of bravado (for it really took courage to stand up to this man whom she felt sure few people dared to oppose) was followed by the relief of the maid's return with the tea tray. It was placed carefully on a sofa table, and again with a bob, and a rather furtive sliding of her gaze over Ynis, the maid withdrew. She had brought two cups and Ynis asked politely if Gard would like a cup of tea.

'I might as well join you.' He sat down and extinguished his cheroot in an ashtray. 'I wish to discuss the wedding.'

The word struck a sense of doom through her heart, and her wrist shook as she poured tea from the silver pot. 'Do you take sugar and cream?' she asked.

'Cream but no sugar.' His tone of voice was dry, as if he sensed very well her reaction to his remark. 'I will also have a scone. My cook, being Cornish, is an excellent one and her scones have been famous since my mother's time.'

Ynis placed one of the warm scones upon a plate and handed it to him. He cut it open and filled it with jam. 'Come, have a scone yourself. You have to get back your strength, and your colour. You have the natural white skin of the Celt, but right now you are looking a positive ghost. Is the prospect of marrying me such an alarming one?'

'You are such a stranger—' She bent her head to her teacup and drank blindly the hot tea, so that it brought quick tears to her eyes. Everything blurred in front of her, as her memory had blurred. If only she dared ask if she had ever loved him! If only she dared hope that he had cared for her. But he gave no sign of it.

'You will soon become used to me – again, and when you marry me the whole of Sea Witch will be yours to share with me. Think of never being homeless, of having dozens of rooms at your disposal, and a strong roof of Cornish slate over your head.'

'Y–you make it sound as if I am marrying you for a home!'

'You are, Ynis. Just as I am marrying you for a son. That was the bargain—'

'But I remember nothing about it,' she broke in. 'You could be inventing every word, for it all sounds unreal to me, and strange, like this room we are sitting in. I feel sure I have never been here before.'

'Drink your tea and eat a scone, and then, Ynis, I will take you to the west wing, to my study, and you will know at once that you have been there before.'

He spoke so decisively that she shrank back in her

chair and the fight ebbed out of her. No man would elaborate such a lie in order to acquire a little nobody for a wife, so it had to be true, this incredible bargain he spoke of.

'Did I – agree to marry you the night I was run down and hurt?' she asked.

'Yes,' he admitted. 'The driver of the car couldn't have seen you, and if he did so he sped on through the night and left you unconscious. It was raining hard when you left Sea Witch, so Doom, my valet, went in my car to find you—'

'Was I running away from you?' She looked directly at him and was met by his inscrutable dark eyes. How dark they were, making him seem almost foreign. His hair, with the deep peak at the centre of his forehead, had a metallic sheen to it because of the silver thread-ing its darkness. His features were emphatic, and the brows above his eyes were like outflung wings, so black, like his lashes, as to be almost exotic.

'You were being rather childish,' he said, as if that explained it all, why she had fled from his house im-mediately after agreeing to become his wife. 'My dear, do stop looking at me as if I'm an ogre who holds you here at my mercy. If you want to walk out on me, then do it now. There is your coat and there is the door. You go straight down the drive and turn to the left to reach the village.'

Her gaze followed the gesture of his left hand at the fur coat and the french doors. A long-fingered, supple hand, whose smallest gesture would at one time have

51

controlled an entire orchestra of musicians; the strings and woodwind, the timpani and side-drum of a full-scale musical storm.

'Would you allow me to go?' she asked tensely.

'No, you little fool, because you have nowhere to go! You belong here and the sooner you accept the fact the more agreeable will the situation be – for both of us.'

Nowhere to go? No people of her own? Nobody but this man who gave her luxury but not a whisper of love?

The situation was not endurable. 'I can't!' She was driven to her feet, into the defensive attitude of a trapped young animal. 'You must be crazy to expect me to carry on with such a – a farce! What sort of a marriage would it be?'

'Much like many another, I expect.' He rose abruptly to his feet and a stride brought him close to her and his arm swept round her and held her. She gave a twist and instantly, with frightening strength, he locked her body against his. 'I have only one arm, but I am not disabled, Ynis. I take, I hold, and you can only hurt yourself if you go on fighting me. The wedding is all arranged and it will take place in three weeks' time. Invitations have been sent out to the few people I require to be present, and a woman is coming down from London to fit your wedding dress. This will be no hole-and-corner affair. You will wear white satin, and we are to be married in church, with choir and bells. No one, here in Cornwall or London, will say that our marriage is one of convenience.'

52

'Do you expect them to believe it a love match?' She stared wildly up at him, her green eyes ablaze with hatred, and helplessness. He was strong and ruthless, and her own body was still weak from her sojourn in bed. She could feel the tremor in her legs and the pounding of her heart. She closed her eyes as her head swam. 'I – I'd like to go back to my room. I feel tired.'

'Then put your arms about my neck.'

'No—'

'Do as I say, Ynis.'

Wearily she obeyed him, and the thought wavered across her mind that he was straight out of Shelley with his brooding power, his pagan face, and his insistence that she obey him. Her fingers clasped nervously the warmth of his neck, and through the flickering of her lashes she saw his face bent to hers, close enough for his breath to stir across her eyelids. She knew that a slight mockery lurked about his mouth and from her own lips came a small gasp as his strong left arm swung her off the ground and he carried her from the lounge to her bedroom. He lowered her to the bed, which in her absence had been smoothly made and the silk bedspread laid across it. For an intent moment Gard held her gaze with his, dominating her, letting her know with that endless look that he intended to abide by everything he had said. The silence was broken from outside, by a knock upon the door that opened on to the hall.

Gard was straightening his tie as the nurse entered. 'There's a long-distance telephone call for you, Mr. St. Clair.' Her eyes flickered from him to Ynis, still in a half-defensive attitude upon the bed, and Ynis wanted to cry out to her to take that silly, knowing look off her face.

'I'm coming.' Gard walked towards the door, looking big and dark and imperturbable; he obviously didn't care a darn what the nurse thought, and when he reached the door he turned to give Ynis his brief flick of a smile. 'I will see you later on, my dear, when you are feeling rested. Perhaps we will have dinner together. *Au'voir* for now.' The door closed behind him and as his footfalls died away, a tremor ran all through Ynis, a combination of relief and fatigue.

The nurse came to her bedside and stood there with that knowing smile as she took the slender wrist and counted the pulse rate. 'Mmm, you are in rather an excitable state. You'd better rest for a while, dearie.'

Ynis snatched her wrist from the warm fingers, and all she wanted was to get away from this house and this impossible situation. 'Nurse, if I ask you to lend me some money, would you do so?'

'A loan, dearie?' The woman ran her inquisitive eyes over the tense young face raised to her. 'And what would it be for — a present for him?'

'Yes — perhaps.' But Ynis was thinking of escape from him, but even as hope lit up her eyes, the voice of common sense spoke a commentary she couldn't ignore. Having made her escape from Sea Witch, where would she go? She had no recollection of her former address, the convent which Gard had told her about, and to find employment she would need an insurance card. The light faded from her eyes and she sank back defeatedly against her pillows and allowed the nurse to remove her shoes. There must be some way, some means of finding that convent...

'Nurse, I must have had a handbag with me when I was run down!' She sat up again, while the nurse tut-tutted as if at the fretful fancies of a child. 'Where is it – where was it put?'

'Really, miss! You'll do yourself no good, getting all het up over a bag. There's only a pound and about thirty pence in it, anyway.'

'I want it!' Ynis was actually trembling and her eyes looked big enough to eat her face. 'Please get it for me!'

The nurse arched an eyebrow and with a rustle of starched skirt she went to the dressing-table and pulled open the top drawer. She took from it a shabby-looking object with a broken clasp and handed it to her patient with a look which implied that such rubbish had no place in such a bedroom.

Ynis took the bag and shot its contents on to the silk bedspread – out tumbled a cheap powder-compact, a religious medal, a purse and a pencil. A quick search of the remaining contents was unrewarding; there was only a handkerchief, a couple of hairclips, and half a packet of mints. Ynis opened the purse and counted the money... all she was worth in the world, a pound note and a handful of coins.

'What were you expecting to find?' Nurse asked.

She glanced up at the nurse and her eyes were suddenly filled with tears. 'I bet, Nurse, that in your handbag you have a few photographs of your family and friends. As you can see, I evidently have no one. No letters ... no address. I'm just a little nobody.'

'With that ring on your finger?' Nurse scoffed. 'In no time at all you'll be a somebody and then you'll have plenty of friends. And you'll have relations. That was Mr. St. Clair's cousin on the phone – Stella Marrick, the West End actress. With any luck she'll be at your wedding and maybe some of her smart friends.'

Ynis wasn't listening ... she was staring at the sapphire ring upon her left hand ... it was worth a lot of money, and if she pawned it, it wouldn't be like stealing it. She could send the ticket to Gard St. Clair, so he could redeem the ring, and the money it fetched would keep her until she regained her memory and could pick up the threads of her former life. It would be better than marrying a man she didn't love, and it would take less courage.

She stared in a kind of fascination at her few possessions on the bed, looking so oddly pathetic against the silk spread, a little haul which told a story of deprivation and the dictates of virtue. Her fingers traced the painted flower on the cheap little compact; she would not have been encouraged by her convent upbringing to use make-up and had only dared to use a dab of powder on her face. She touched the profile of the saint on the religious medal and felt a tremor in her fingers. She had obviously been taught to be honest and to respect the property of other people, yet she must use the ring to get away from Gard! She couldn't marry him, for his purpose was a sinister one, and she sensed it with all her being.

She replaced her things in the shabby little bag and noted once again that she didn't possess a key, which could only mean that the one truth he had told her was that she was homeless.

'I will rest for an hour or two,' she said. 'I want to regain my strength as soon as possible.'

'Of course you do, dearie.' The nurse gave her a rather coy smile. 'Cook has been given orders to start baking your wedding cake, which must mean that Mr. St. Clair is impatient to be wed. I reckon he feels he's waited long enough to become a family man. It's such a shame—' She broke off and skimmed a look over the slim, tousle-haired figure on the bed. Her smile was significant. 'He must have been a fine figure of a man before that accident to his arm, and they say that beauty doesn't like imperfection. Beauty likes its match.'

'Are you hinting, Nurse, that some beautiful woman walked out on him when he lost his arm?' Ynis asked mildly.

'His cousin, so they say. Stella Marrick.' The nurse was staring at Ynis as if for some sign of jealousy, but she only let her head droop on the pillow and held the shabby bag against her cheek.

57

'Stella – Star,' she murmured, and like a weary child she drifted off to sleep, holding the bag as if it were a reassurance and a shield.

CHAPTER FOUR

A WEEK later the nurse left Sea Witch, and Ynis breathed a sigh of relief. She was now feeling much better, though her mind was still unwilling to reveal what it was hiding.

She felt sure it was something she didn't truly wish to remember, because it would hurt her, and each time she took tea with Gard, or dined with him, she was tensed for the sudden stab of recollection, the bringing into real focus the face she saw 'as through a glass darkly'.

In the meantime she made herself acquainted with the house, whose lawns stretched to old grey walls that held back the moors, and whose long west terrace overlooked the ocean. She met some of the people who worked on the estate, and she knew what they were thinking when they turned to stare after her slight young figure; she was a foreigner among them, and hardly suited to be the mistress of a big house that was of importance to the community.

The valet, Doom, had the oddest way of looking at her, as if he regarded her as a stray cat rather than his master's bride-to-be.

One morning, finding her astray among the many winding passages of Sea Witch, he guided her back to the morning-room with the solemn air of a man who knew many things and spoke of them rarely. 'Doom,' she said suddenly, 'if you hadn't found me that night I might have died.'

'You might well have done so, miss,' he agreed, without a change of expression on the long face which she was discovering was deceptively severe.

'I am very grateful to you for coming out in the rain to find me.'

'It was the master who ordered out the car and said I must look for you, miss.'

'It was he who made me dash off into the darkness and the rain!'

'I wouldn't know about that, miss. It is not my place to discuss it.'

'You will stay loyal to the last breath, Doom.' She smiled a little and gazed into the fire with her slanting green eyes, almost akin to the young cat curled upon a stool near the warmth – Topaz, who disdained any touch but that of her master's lean hand.

'Have you been many years at Sea Witch?' Ynis glanced up at Doom inquiringly.

'I have been here just on five years, miss,' he replied. 'I came from the apartment in London with Mr. St. Clair, when he decided to live in the country at his family home.'

'Then you worked for him before—' She hesitated, but knew that she had to pry if she was to learn anything valid. 'You were his valet at the time of the accident, weren't you, Doom?'

'Yes, miss.' His voice became remote and he turned

to face the door. 'If there is anything you require, then I will send Alice to you.'

'Doom,' a note of entreaty came into her voice, 'if all of you shut me out, then I shall never remember the details of my own meeting with Mr. St. Clair, and why I ran away from him that night. Tell me, was I afraid of him because of his amputation?'

The valet turned again to look at her and a flicker of some emotion – perhaps sympathy – showed in his eyes. 'I have orders not to discuss the matter, as you will understand, miss, the subject is painful to the master. He was world known, and he lived for his work and his music.'

'And that is all you dare tell me?' she murmured.

'Yes, miss.' He bowed his head and something of fear seemed to mingle with his almost Edwardian air of dignity. 'That is all I dare to say. You wish for coffee and biscuits?'

'No – yes, I might as well have something to pass the time. I see that it's begun to drizzle with rain.' She stared at the wide windows and beyond them to a vista of rain-misted lawns and azalea bushes of so deep a crimson that they looked like bonfires. 'This is a very large and impressive house, Doom. It must seem like a joke to you and the other members of the staff that I am to be its mistress?'

'I don't permit the staff to discuss the matter in my presence, miss. Mr. St. Clair has his reasons, I daresay. He's human enough to feel lonely.' Doom swept open the door, brusquely, as if he had spoken indiscreetly.

'I will send Alice along with your coffee, miss.'

She watched as the door closed behind him, and his reference to Gard's loneliness seemed to be left and shut in with her, like a reproach. She paced the room, a slim, tense figure in tapered slacks and a moss-green sweater. She wanted to walk on the moors, but knew already from Alice, a local girl, that when it drizzled with rain an opaque mist sometimes settled down over the moorland and made it treacherous for the person who had not been brought up to know its secrets and its vagaries. The stranger could be pixy-led, Alice had told her, right into a bog that even on a grey day had a deceptive, pretty green look.

She gave a start as the door opened and Alice came into the morning-room. 'Your coffee, Miss Ynis, and hot biscuits straight out of the oven. Cook says you need fattening up.'

'For the wedding feast?' Ynis had to make a joke of it, at least with Alice, who was young like herself and not quite so critical-looking as Mrs. Walker the house-keeper, or Brown who always seemed to be cleaning the windows and polishing the furniture. Most of the staff had that air of having been at Sea Witch since Gard was a boy, and it was natural enough that they should take a proprietorial interest in his affairs.

'I have a feeling, Alice, that I'm one of those people who stay lean all their lives.' Ynis sat down in one of the deep window seats and had the tray put beside her. 'Did you see your boy-friend last night?'

'Yes, Miss Ynis.' Alice smiled with the assurance of

the pretty, slightly plump girl who had no trouble finding love. 'We went dancing and I wore my new blue dress, and there was a pop group there—'

'A what?' Ynis broke in. 'Whatever's a pop group?'

'Don't you know, miss?' Alice looked quite astounded. 'They're a group of boys who play and sing the latest hit tunes. I'll put the radio on and you'll get some idea of what I mean.' The young maid went to the long wall adjacent to the fireplace, where a combined cabinet held a television set and a radiogram. She began to turn knobs and various snatches of music invaded the room. Ynis watched and listened, and could hardly believe her ears when a raucous male voice suddenly filled the room with the most awful sound of pain, as if he were being beaten over the head while an electric organ played an accompaniment. Alice turned to her with a smile, which quickly froze on her face as the terrace doors swept open and Gard St. Clair came into the room. There was rain on his black hair, and thunder on his brow.

'By heaven!' he exclaimed. 'Whatever barbaric rubbish are you listening to, Ynis? Turn it off at once, Alice!'

'Yes, sir.' The young maid obeyed him promptly and hurried from the room as fast as her feet could carry her.

'What a cacophony!' Gard stared hard at Ynis. 'Is that your idea of music? If it is my girl, then you're going to have to change your taste because I won't allow in this house such an assault on the eardrums and the sensibilities.'

'Alice was trying to explain pop music to me and she thought if I heard some of it—' Ynis broke off and had to laugh at the outraged look on Gard's face. 'I'm sorry. I realize that you must admire only the very best music, and I must admit that I didn't much care for that vocal demonstration.'

'I should think not!' Gard flung himself down on the big leather couch and his left hand reached for a panatella out of the box on the low table. 'If that's coffee then I'll join you for a cup.'

'Yes, it's freshly made.' She went to the bell and rang it. Alice reappeared, looking rather subdued, and Ynis gave her a little half-wink as she asked for another cup and saucer.

'You did jump down the poor girl's throat,' Ynis said, as she poured the coffee and handed him the cup. His panatella rested on the edge of the ashtray and sent up a thin stream of aromatic smoke, and he quirked an eyebrow at Ynis as he stirred his coffee. Half-turned like that, with his grey jacket open, his empty sleeve could not be seen. He wore a black cashmere sweater rolled at the throat, and his rain-ruffled hair gave him a slightly raffish look. In that instant, caught as if by a camera, Ynis saw him as he had been when music ruled his life, and both his supple hands ruled an entire orchestra. It was disturbing, that brief glimpse of the younger Gard St. Clair; the one with the world in his two hands, with a brilliant future ahead of him.

She glanced away from him, at a picture on the wall, as she sipped her coffee.

'I forget how young you are,' he drawled, 'and that you must have friends of your own age to converse with. Well, my cousin will be arriving at Sea Witch this evening and she will be bringing her young secretary with her, and also a young man who writes plays. We shall have company, Ynis, and I shall expect you to act as if you can't wait to become my wife.'

'You mean,' her green eyes clashed with his, 'I must fall all over you, merely to prove to your cousin Stella that she isn't the great love of your life? You see, I'm not totally ignorant of your reasons for this marriage, Gard.'

'It would seem not.' His eyes bored into hers, black as the sweater against the brown skin of his throat, and with a silky sheen of deep, rather cynical amusement. 'So you've been listening to the gossip of the maids, or that rather inquisitive nurse, and you've come up with some romantic theory of your own, is that it? You think I'd marry just anyone in order to spite Stella? The idea will amuse her, if it occurs to her. I doubt if she'd feel flattered.'

'Meaning she's beautiful and I'm plain,' Ynis threw at him.

'Plain spoken, at least,' he murmured, and a gibing little smile flickered on his lips. 'Are you trying for a compliment, my dear? Well, you don't have to try too hard. Your eyes are green without a dash of hazel in them, and you're young, and virtuous as that convent you came from. If you imagine these things aren't exciting to a man, then let me assure you they are. By the way, I'm thirty-six, and I can't pretend to be virtuous, but all that is past and you will help to bury it.'

'You mean Stella, your career, and travelling all over the world?'

'I mean exactly all those things, Ynis. The old life is severed, just like my arm, and with you I begin a different life.'

'You don't love me,' she said quietly. 'I – I couldn't forget that even if I forgot other things. At least my heart wouldn't. I want to know why I ran away from you that night!'

'We had a foolish argument, my dear. You smashed a valuable ornament in my study, and I told you not to behave like a child. After all, where will you go, what else is there, if you don't marry me? I am all you have, really.'

'Really?' she echoed. 'You say that as if – oh, I don't know. As if there might be someone whom you judge as insignificant. If there is someone, then you have no right to keep me in the dark.'

'As your fiancé I have certain rights and I intend to impose them.' He held out his cup for a refill, and there was in the gesture more than a hint of dominance. 'The right to act in your best interest became mine when my ring became yours. Do you understand me, Ynis?'

'Your meaning is very clear, Gard. You sound as if you intend to bully me.' She lifted the coffee pot and saw reflected in the silver surface her own white face, and the storm-green of her eyes. 'You've said already that I must like your kind of music, so I gather that applies to everything. I must let you dictate to me, or else!'

'Yes, I intend to guide your taste in certain matters, but I shan't box your ears in the process. I am not that sadistic, Ynis, so don't give me a martyred look with my coffee. Thank you.' He sat back with his cup, and there was a tiny twist to his lip. 'I can't help but wonder if your upbringing among all those saintly women has given you the idea that marriage is a sort of torment, to be borne like thorns instead of kisses. I hope you know the facts of life, or must I teach you those as I teach you the facts of music and art?'

She flushed slightly, for his eyes had narrowed so that his lashes met and gave him a subtle and considering look, one that took her in from her ankles to her lips. There was nothing about Gard that was remotely monkish, and even the loss of an arm did not reduce his masculine quality. He might not feel for her the tender aspects of love, but he meant to be her lover when their marriage took place. He had already stated his terms . . . she needed a home, and he wanted a son. The demand was there in his eyes. A dark-eyed perfect son to compensate for his own imperfection.

Ynis felt shaken . . . if she had loved him she might have given him anything, her heart and all her youthful willingness to learn from him, but she felt only fear when she looked at him. He had only to lean forward to snatch her from her chair, and the threat of this slumbered in his eyes as she sat there as tensed as a willow-branch in the wind, ready to leap out of reach at his slightest movement.

Suddenly he laughed, a deep sound in his throat, mocking her for the blazing green rejection of her eyes. 'Relax, my little witch. I don't intend to be hated by you even if you find it impossible to love me. What kind of a marriage would it be if I couldn't win even your toleration? Having now seen something of Sea Witch, I hope you are prepared to tolerate its master?'

She felt the intensity of his gaze as he spoke, and she sensed that for him she had an enigmatic quality. Other women he had known would have been worldly like himself, but she came from a convent, and there was every likelihood that he was the only man who had ever been close to her. Her gaze darted, swift as a dragonfly wing, across the bold, hard line of his lips. Had he ever kissed her? How strange that she could not remember what it had felt like, that dark face bent close to hers while his lips took a kiss. He would have taken . . . she felt utterly certain that she had never given in to him.

'Why are you looking at me like that?' he asked curiously. 'What are you thinking – that I am older than you, and not half so romantic as you would like me to be?'

'Your eyes are so – so domineering,' she shot back at him. 'You have always had your own way, haven't you? All your life. You don't like to be thwarted.'

'And do you intend to thwart me?' Suddenly, just as

68

she had visualized it, he reached out and the strength in his left hand was almost inhuman as he gripped her wrist and pulled her relentlessly to the couch where he sat. She half fell across his knees and to steady herself she clutched at his right shoulder and felt with horror the emptiness where the flesh and bone and muscles had once been, there beneath the pinned sleeve. She gave a little gasp and the horror was still in her eyes as they fastened on his face, and then as if he had to blot out that look he swiftly bent his head and his mouth crushed hers, deliberately, without tenderness or even the hunger of desire. It was a punishment far more effective than a blow, the sudden shocking intimacy of his lips forcing hers to yield, to part for him, until the room was reeling, and nerves deep beneath her skin were alive as never before. She hadn't known, she hadn't been taught that sensation could be so clamouring, so overriding, so self-destroying.

'Don't ...' She twisted free of his mouth and her face buried itself against the shoulder that was armless. 'Not like that!'

'How, my dear?' His laughter was softly taunting against the side of her neck. 'Kisses on the wrist and old-time wooing happen only in books, and you have to become used to me, and I'm really not so bad as a nasty dose of medicine, am I? Are you such a child that I have to be taken with a shudder?'

'If only I knew you better—' Again a tremor shook her and she felt the pressure of his fingers against her waist, holding her to him in a kind of curiosity mingled with a little cruelty. She was his and he had no intention of saying otherwise; of letting her go. He didn't care a rap that she found him more fearful than fascinating. He seemed to her to enjoy the fear which she felt.

'There are certain terrors known only to a girl,' he said. 'The fact is fascinating to a man, and that's the bare truth. My dear girl, you have to learn about life sooner or later, and better to do so with me than some young clerk or student who can give you only a couple of rented rooms, a bathroom shared with other people, and a worried, fretful look before you're thirty. Believe me, I shall take a pride in that clear-skinned, leggy virtue of yours. Already I'm planning to give you a colt and to have you taught riding, and I want to have you painted by Bart Spearman, a primitive artist of no mean talent, who might capture that wild and innocent look you have in those green eyes. I shall make you the most envied woman in the West Country. No one shall pity you for being married to three-quarters of a man!'

He put her away from him and rose to his feet. He went and stood in front of the window, framed big and dark, and painfully savage about the mouth. 'Does it sicken you, Ynis, the thought of seeing me without a sweater and a jacket to hide my amputation? They did a neat job, I assure you.' He swung towards the window and his hand reached for the handle. 'Stella should arrive with her escort some time this evening. I understand they are driving down from London, so there will be no need for them to be met at the station. Mrs. Walker will see to their rooms, so all you need do is to wear a pretty dress and try to look as though I plan to wed you, not to eat you. Do you hear?'

'Yes, Gard, I'm not deaf.' She glared at him. 'Perhaps you would like to choose the dress I should wear. One that will impress your cousin sufficiently to believe that you care for a plain little nobody who knows nothing of your world.'

'Stella has imagination,' he drawled. 'She may realize that it's your unworldly quality which intrigues me. And I may accept your invitation to come and choose your dress . . . how does it feel for a little nobody to own a wardrobe of day and evening clothes?'

'Decadent,' she said, 'despite your generosity in providing them.'

'Your trousseau, my child, and don't be so outspoken.' He quirked a black eyebrow so that it almost met the dark peak of hair that gave him such a devilish look. 'A man likes a little more subtlety in his bride-to-be, and don't pretend that it doesn't feel good to wear good clothes after those rags they took off you at the hospital. I had them burned and I had every stitch replaced by one of the best dress houses in London. A proper sort of girl would thank me.'

'Thank you,' she said ungraciously. 'People can't help being poor, you know. It's no disgrace.'

'You'd prefer to be ungraceful when Stella comes to look you over?' he mocked. 'My cousin is sables and sorcery on a grand scale, and by heaven, you'll look good tonight or I'll tan that innocent backside of yours!' With these words he left her, closing the french window behind him and casting her a threatening look before he went on his way along the rainswept terrace. She could hear the wind, and with a little shiver she went closer to the fire, and after a moment she knelt there staring at the flames as they licked about the logs. In this room, where the furniture was more comfortable than grand, the fire was a real one and every now and again a spot of rain sizzled down the chimney.

So Stella was coming today, and she must act the starry-eyed bride-to-be. It would be impossible, and she hated the rain that was keeping her at Sea Witch when she longed to get away. She ran to the window and saw that a foot of mist was creeping over the lawns. Over the moors the mist would be thicker, drifting on to the road that led to the village. She must be patient and wait for a fine day; a day when Gard was absent from the house, and wouldn't know she was gone until it was too late to fetch her back.

She heard the door open and turned to look. It was Alice, and as she picked up the coffee tray to take it to the kitchen she cast a demurely questioning look at Ynis.

'No more pop music, I think, Alice.' Ynis said it lightly, for it mustn't look as if she took sides against Gard. He was the master of this house, and one to be held in awe if not in affection. 'Mr. St. Clair is keenly fond of serious music and doesn't care for all that caterwauling. Is it really all that popular?'

'Among young people, Miss Ynis.' Alice looked put out by the description, and she left the room with a flounce. Ynis gave a little shrug; soon she would disentangle herself from the people at Sea Witch and the emotional cross-currents which kept a household humming, from below stairs to the master bedroom. How strange that an entire house, and a big one at that, should revolve around the personality of one man, attuned to his slightest wish and desire, its routine thrown out of gear if he should suddenly charge out as dinner was being served in that grand dining-room, and decide to picnic on the lawn. She gave a slight laugh, and absorbed the quietness that lay like velvet over the twittering of birds in the almost soundless rain, and somewhere in the hall the sound of an electric cleaner mowing the dust from the big carpets.

Suddenly a man laughed and the sound startled her, and then she realized that it was Brown out there in the hall, probably flirting with Alice.

What did it feel like, Ynis wondered, to be flirted with and admired by a young man? She felt utterly certain that Gard St. Clair was the only man who had ever taken any interest in her, and why he should do so was a mystery. She walked to a scrolled mirror on the panelled wall and stared at herself in the large reflective oval entwined with silvery serpents, their forked tongues licking at silver leaves.

He had said that her eyes were those of a young witch, and that her skin was white. Too white, she thought, making her hair seem dark in contrast. She liked fair-haired people . . . yes, strange how she knew that without being able to recall a single face or voice from her previous life. Strange that the little quirks and fancies of one's personality could be stronger than memory.

She took her hair in her fists and bunched it at the crown of her head, intensifying the fine-boned structure of her face and the sensitive width of her mouth. She wasn't in the least pretty, but she supposed there was a certain witchery about her green eyes shaded by thick dark lashes that cast little shadows when she blinked against the whiteness of her skin. With a shrug she released her hair to the line of her jaw, and told herself that Stella Marrick was in for a surprise. The actress must be very curious about Gard's prospective bride if she was taking the trouble to drive all the way from London to his house on the Cornish coast.

A look of mutiny stole into the green eyes that gazed back at Ynis from the mirror . . . she resented the part which Gard expected her to play in front of his beautiful cousin. He had ordered her to look nice and to pretend she loved him. How did she do that, by throwing her arms about his neck and snuggling up to him? Was that what he wanted, a young and ardent shield against the woman who had wanted a lionized conductor, not a man with one arm?

He had looked bitter when he had asked her if she found the thought of his amputation sickening, as if now he judged the reaction of all women by the reaction of his cousin. Stella must have shrunk from him,

74

and he couldn't forget that, or forgive it, and Ynis felt a stirring of compassion as she recalled the proud, harsh look of him when he had stood by the window, framed by the sea light which seemed to fill the sky over Sea Witch, and made a cleaving motion down his right side with his strong left hand.

He had called himself three-quarters of a man, and he wanted to show the arrogant Stella that another girl, a much more youthful one, found him desirable and forceful despite the imperfection which Stella had rejected. But didn't he realize what Stella would think? She would judge Ynis as a plain little nobody, ready to throw herself at any man for the sake of a wedding ring. She would be scornful, and see through the falsity of any show of affection Ynis might make towards Gard. Ynis stared at her own reflected image . . . Stella probably meant to break up the marriage before it even took place, for beautiful actresses were usually spoiled and though they might wilfully break a man's heart they didn't like others to come along who might mend it.

Ynis sighed and felt as if all this meditation was making her head spin. She wandered from the morning-room into the hall belonging to the south side of the house. Here the walls were sea-blue, with a pale blue and green ceiling, where on slender steel chains hung the crystal buds and blooms of chandeliers that tinkled very faintly in the wind rising from the sea and the moors. As she listened to that soft tinkling it took on the quality of the faint, faint laughter of a pretty ghost.

Along the walls ran white mouldings of garlands, and shells and sea-horses, and in the centre of the hall stood a giant vase on a pedestal of white marble, from the mouth of which burst purple and green foliage.

From the start, from the moment Ynis had left her bedroom to start exploring Sea Witch, it had been a lovely shock to find such rooms set within a house of grey moorland stone, high-walled and turreted like castle of the moors. Rooms so graceful they held her in thrall, so that it was no longer possible to believe the lie which Gard had told her ... such decorations had never been meant for a little nobody. They had been designed to show off the beauty of a certain woman ... a theatrical woman, with a drama to her looks, like that great white urn of deep lilac flower, the gloss of long silken curtains at the circular windows of the glassed-in tower at the end of the hall, the softly fused glow of sea colour ... blue-green as the sapphire on Ynis's left hand.

Long before some crisis in her life, which she could not yet recall, had brought her to this house, this ring and these rooms had been meant for Stella. A perfect background for her beauty, which she had rejected, and which Ynis must also reject. Far from being loved too much, she wasn't loved at all, and even the siren call of Sea Witch must not entice her into a loveless marriage.

The moorland wind shook the windows of the glass tower, and again the crystal buds of the chandeliers tinkled overhead, like the faint and mocking laughter of a ghost.

Ynis locked her hands together, hiding the ring beneath her clenched fingers. But Stella was not a ghost ... she was very much alive, and within the next few hours she would return to Sea Witch.

CHAPTER FIVE

YNIS had no intention of taking seriously Gard's remark about choosing the dress she should wear for her first meeting with Stella, and she was in her bedroom, standing barefoot at the sliding cupboard, her hair still tied at the crown of her head from her bath, when he entered her room from the terrace.

She swung round startled and blinked at the darkness of him, and the distinction in a well-cut dinner jacket, white ruffled shirt, and narrow dark trousers that made him seem extra tall.

'What do you want?' She clutched at her robe and felt intolerably undressed as Gard's eyes swept over her.

He came towards her across the thick pale carpet, silent as the smile that mocked her from the depths of his eyes. 'My dear, you invited me to come and valet you,' he drawled. 'Did you imagine I'd forgo the pleasure and send young Alice to you? That girl would encourage you to wear a plunge neckline and a pair of false eyelashes. Now don't back away from me as if I'm about to outrage your virtue . . . as if I would when you look like a small girl who has just climbed out of the bath and is ready to be told a story on her daddy's knee.'

But as he spoke these words his face underwent a

curious change; she saw the tightening of his jaw muscles and the dangerous narrowing of his eyelids. His left hand reached brusquely into her wardrobe and hangers rattled as he pushed the dresses from side to side. His hand bunched a frothy skirt, then dismissed it for something silvery, until finally he drew forth a pale violet tube of silk, so simple as to be plain, and so soft that he could have crushed it almost to nothing in his hand.

'This is the one,' he said, handing it to her.

She took it reluctantly and stood there like his audience as he reached down into the shoe rack and selected a pair of pale violet shoes.

'The outrageous combination of green eyes, white skin, and violet silk should create quite a sensation, Ynis.' He looked her over once again, his eyes still narrowed and flickering in that oddly tempered way, as if he too were strung up. 'Put the dress on, and please do something about your hair.'

'You're a bossy devil,' she retorted. 'I don't like the dress. It isn't my sort of dress at all.'

'What would you know about that?' he said sardonically. 'The garment is cut by a master hand, and you have exactly the slender shape for it, and you'll look more of a young witch than ever wearing it. What about make-up? Did they supply some with the clothes? I told the shop you were to have everything a young woman would need, being so far from London.'

'I don't wear make-up.' She thought of the cheap

79

little compact in the handbag which was all that was left of what she had been wearing and carrying the night of her accident. 'I'm not an actress, remember.'

'You are being impudent because you're nervous.' He walked to the dressing-table and opened several of the drawers. Ynis knew he would find the make-up box which she had put there, filled with its little boxes and phials and lipsticks, all designed to enhance subtly the contours and the features of the plainest face. She hadn't a clue as to how all that magic worked, and she felt resentful because Gard seemed to want to make of her a substitute for the glamorous Stella.

'I imagine you're entirely ignorant of cosmetics,' he said. 'Well, all you really need is face powder and lipstick, and a touch of eye-shadow, and you should manage to apply those without making yourself look a clown.'

'Does it matter, Gard?' she asked, staring him in the face. 'Your cousin is a woman of the world and she won't be fooled into thinking that you're crazy about me.'

'What makes you so certain that I'm not crazy about you, Ynis?' That mocking note was in his voice, but his gaze as it travelled over her was slow and lazy, and shaded by his eyelashes. 'Your amnesia has shut the door on certain memories, and I'd hardly be marrying you if you didn't make some appeal to my emotions.'

'Those emotions bruised by Stella?' she asked. 'Secondhand emotions, Gard? Good enough for the little nobody who has always been accustomed to hand-me-downs.'

'My dear, you said it, not I.' His drawl was far more insolent than anything she could have managed. 'I'll go and wait for you in your sitting-room while you dress yourself, and don't forget the touch of make-up. A woman looks undressed at dinner without it.' He opened the door of the adjoining room and went inside, and as the door closed behind him Ynis flung the violet-coloured dress on to the bed, and with mutiny burning in her eyes she turned to the wardrobe and snatched from the rail a white dress with a bodice of closely patterned lace.

Fifteen minutes later she was ready. Her hair was neatly combed, her lips were bright, and temper had lit her eyes so there was no need to apply a cosmetic to them. She walked into the sitting-room in her silver kid sandals and found Gard seated in one of the winged chairs in a lush old-gold velvet. It was a comfortable but exotic little room, with a bearskin rug across the floor, and a velvet swing-seat in the glassed-in balcony.

Gard raised his eyes from the bearskin rug and his thoughts must have been far away, for he seemed to look right through her. She stood braced by the door in the white dress, and she defied him with a flexible tilting of her head to unzip the dress and drag it off her back. Their eyes duelled for several silent moments, then abruptly he laughed, deeply in his throat.

'You are right after all, Ynis,' he said, rising to his

feet, like a dark tower in that gold and glass room! 'You do know which type of dress suits you best.'

She sank back against the door with a sigh of relief. 'I can't pretend to be sophisticated, Gard.'

'It would seem not.' He came across to her, very tall as he stood close and gazed down at her. He touched her hair with his hand, letting his fingers feel its soft texture. His gaze moved to the tiny nerve that beat visibly under the pale skin of her neck. 'I have something to give you . . . a trinket from the family safe, so there's no need for you to go all tense with rejection.'

He slid his hand into the pocket of his dinner jacket and took from it a chain holding a single pearl in a filigree setting. 'You had better put it on, Ynis. I can't fasten it for you.' He pressed the chain and jewel into her hand. 'I know there's a superstition about pearls, but it's only a single teardrop.'

The pearl clung in the strands of woven gold, and the chain was so fine it might have been woven by a spider. She could't refuse to wear the trinket, but her hands shook a little as she fastened it around her neck and felt the touch of it against her skin.

'And now let me have a look at you.' He drew her under the light, clasping the side of her waist with his hand, and he inspected her closely from her silver sandals and upwards to her wide green eyes. 'You pay for dressing, Ynis, as they say. Quite a transformation from the little waif to my future wife. And now shall we go and say hello to Stella?'

'If we must,' she said, and felt the nip of his fingers as

he led her to the door and out on to the hall, where the chandeliers were alight, great glistening jewels that gave the place a party look. They crossed to the drawing-room, where he paused for a moment to give her a slightly warning look. 'It's all right, Gard.' She touched the pearl at her throat. 'I shall try not to let you down, but it is a little ironical for your future wife to be meeting your past love. Why, it's rather like a play, complete with lovely star and slightly nervous ingénue, not to mention the tall, dark hero.'

His look, as he took in these words, was quizzical. 'For a young convent girl you seem to have absorbed some odd facts and fancies.'

'Don't forget, Gard, that the bedroom I occupy here at Sea Witch is well stocked with books, and I have discovered that I like reading in bed. I have recently read the autobiography of another leading actress, so I wouldn't appear too ignorant of the world in front of Stella Marrick.'

'The word of stage people, my child, is a raffishly romantic one. They dramatize the slightest incident, and are gay, jealous, and nearly always fascinating.' He threw open the door of the drawing-room as he spoke, and even before Ynis entered the lovely royal-blue room with its soft touches of grey and its silver-hooded wall-lights, she caught the sound of a woman's voice, and heard plainly what was said.

'I know you think me awful, Pierre, because I gossip with the maids, but one hears such useful snippets of information. The girl let out to me, quite innocently, that the little upstart has never lived in a house like this before, or known the kind of life which we call ladylike. She has wormed her way in, and somehow she has got a ring on her hand. If he intends to marry her, then he's doing it out of pique—'

There the voice broke off and the woman in the sapphire velvet, with her bare smooth shoulders to the door, stood for seconds staring silently at the man who stood facing her. His good-looking face expressed too late a look of warning, and then with the outrageous poise of the actress Stella swung round, and stood there all in blue gazing at Gard St. Clair with large eyes that matched the colour of her gown.

'My dears, you have just caught me rehearsing a few lines from Pierre's new play. You know what we people are! We take our work wherever we go – Gard, darling, how are you? I've so looked forward to seeing you.' She came across to him, the long full skirt of her wonderful velvet dress trailing across the grey carpet, and Ynis, with a little twitch to her lip, decided that Stella Marrick was very accomplished in her art, and not so much beautiful as striking. She had a strong-boned, arrogantly assured face, framed by titian-red hair centrally parted and coiled into a chignon at the nape of her neck. Her figure was superb, and diamonds blazed in her ear-lobes against the dramatic colour of her hair. Another diamond blazed in the cleavage of her dress, throwing its facets on to the smooth pallor of her skin.

She seemed quite tall until she reached Gard, and

even she had to look up to him, and her scarlet lips seemed poised for his kiss.

'How are you, Stella?' Very suavely he took her hand and kissed the back of that instead of her waiting lips. 'I'm sorry I wasn't here to greet you, but I had some business to attend to at one of the farms. I hope Mrs. Walker has made you comfortable?'

'Gard, darling, how formal you sound! Don't forget that I very nearly grew up in this house and I hate to be spoken to like any ordinary guest.' The blue eyes flashed to Ynis and the scarlet lips smiled. 'And is this the little girl you are going to marry? All in white – how sweet! There is nothing like a rehearsal before the actual performance.'

'Yes, Stella, this is my fiancée.' His voice grated. 'Ynis, meet my friend, Miss Marrick, whom the stage critics applaud for her gift of insinuation amounting almost to insult. She has been so spoiled by the adulation of her adoring public that she believes she can say and do exactly as she wishes – without retaliation. Don't allow her to intimidate you.'

'Really, Gard!' Stella gave him a wounded look. 'You make me sound a virago, and you will have this child on the defensive with me when I hope to become such friends with her. Ynis! What an unusual name. I could declare you invented it, but of course you didn't?'

'No, Miss Marrick.' Ynis met the eyes that matched the ring on the third finger of *her* left hand; sapphire blue, artistically shaded and with lashes so long they almost looked artificial. 'Unless it was invented for me. I expect you know that I have a slight amnesia and can't quite recall the past. Gard probably told you when he spoke to you on the telephone.'

'Gard, dear child, merely told me that he was getting married and I might care to come and meet the bride-to-be.' The dramatic eyes sharpened until they were like blue diamonds in that face so full of expression and yet which gave nothing away of the woman. She looked and reacted and seemed all actress; as clever, perhaps, as Gard at hiding what her true feelings were, and they could have been feelings of hate for the bride-to-be, and a love that still smouldered for the man she had hurt and who now retaliated in an ancient yet very effective way . . . by confronting her with a young rival.

'Amnesia sounds very uncomfortable, or very convenient.' Stella's smile was so charming it was almost believable. 'Pierre, do come on over and meet this un-usual girl, who dresses as girls used to dress, and whose mind has a fascinating veil over it. I'm so intrigued that I think I shall get Pierre to write me a play around the subject. He's from Brittany, you know, and they're as subtle as the Cornish.'

He came out from the alcove where Ynis had been aware of him watching the interchange between Stella and herself. His hair was thick and silver-fair and deep in the slate-grey of his eyes there burned a little laughter. He wore a maharajah jacket in thick black silk, buttoned to the neck with a row of small gleaming buttons. Like Stella he was theatrical, but unlike the actress he had a quirk of humour to his mouth as if he regarded life as a game rather than people as opponents to be outwitted or outrageously flattered.

'I am charmed to know you.' His voice and his accent were attractive, and he appraised her in a different way from Gard, who seemed all the time to treat her like a Galatea who must learn to be faultless in dress and manner. Pierre Dumont's glance dwelt a moment on her mouth, as if for him the shape and youthful texture of her lips were more important than the dress she wore. Something gleamed in his eyes . . . surprise, and a hint of intrigue.

It was he who took Ynis in to dinner, while Stella went in with Gard, looking so glamorous beside him, and so assured, as if she had already reclaimed his heart and had no intention of taking seriously his engagement to Ynis. He had always been hers to charm or wound, and the look she slanted at Ynis across the flower-decked dining-table was lazily malicious.

'Are you allowed wine?' she drawled, as Doom waited at table and poured the pale gold wine into the stemmed glasses after Gard had tasted it to his satisfaction.

'Don't be kittenish, Stella.' It was Pierre who spoke. 'Ynis is not a child and you know it, *chérie.*'

'Trust a Frenchman to see beneath the limpid surface.' Stella ran a polished fingernail down her jaw, lazily aware that the movement directed the gaze to the smooth line of her cheek and chin. The smile she gave

Gard was full of secrets. 'Do you remember my coming out party, when we ran off with a bottle of champagne and got so beautifully tipsy down on the beach? There was everyone looking for us, and we were all alone and making the most of my status as a fully-fledged adult. Of course, in this permissive age girls don't wait for the key of the door ... mmm, what delicious pheasant *en casserole*! It was always a favourite dish of mine, and you know, don't you, Gard, that I never lose my desire for what I love.'

'There are two subjects,' said Pierre, his wine glass in his hand, 'which our divine Stella must discuss at least twice a day. One is the theatre and her status as a queen at its court, and the other is the splendours and the savageries of love.' He raised his wine glass to Stella in a slightly taunting way. 'Your health and happiness, *chérie*. May you always star in my plays, but never in my love life.'

'French *savant*,' she retorted. 'Love for you is the bee and the flower. You flit, Pierre, and taste the honey without ever getting stung yourself. One fine day, *mon ami*, you will be taken unaware by one of these little distractions, and then, perhaps, you might write for me something more subtle than a dazzling comedy of errors.'

'*Touché*,' he laughed, and seemed unstung by her cruel and uncaring tongue. He winked at Ynis, then glanced inquiringly at Gard. 'After this most excellent dinner, *m'sieur*, may I take your fiancée to show me your garden by moonlight? I have heard much of Sea

88

Witch, and as a writer I wish to absorb some of its witchery.'

'You may of course allow Ynis to show you around,' Gard said suavely, the glimmer of the table candle-flames reflecting in his eyes as they flicked the face of the girl beside Pierre, the pallor of her dress a contrast to his dark jacket with a sheen to it. 'But don't forget that she is not of your world and that she lived an enclosed life before I took her over.'

'Darling,' laughed Stella, 'you sound more like her guard than her lover! Ynis, do beware of Pierre. He has flirted with my secretary and made the poor girl so miserable that she refused to come on this trip. Young girls just won't believe that he's a confirmed bachelor of the art of making love, and when they learn the truth, it's tears and sulks for those for whom they work. Do think twice before allowing this child into his clutches, Gard.'

'Well, *m'sieur*?' Gard was looking straight at Pierre, and his dark features were stamped with that relentless quality that always made Ynis shiver a little when she encountered it. 'Must I think twice before trusting you with Ynis? Down here in Cornwall we are still a little feudal in our ways, and our women are sacrosanct. I might kill the man who took the innocence out of those green eyes.'

'*Ah, non—*' Pierre gave a rather unbelieving laugh. 'Do you mean it, I wonder? *Ce n'est pas sérieux?*'

'Every word,' said Gard, calmly eating the straw-berry mousse which had just been served by his manservant, on whose dour face not a flicker of surprise showed as Gard made his pronouncement.

'*Très bien*.' Pierre shrugged, half with humour, and half with the acceptance of a man who knows that the other man means what he says and isn't joking. His eyebrow was quirked as he regarded the Cornishman. 'I believe this part of England has many surprising elements, not the least of them that *à la coeur pur* still exists.'

'And has to be protected,' Gard murmured, wiping his lips on his table napkin and looking at Ynis for a brief but intense moment. 'Also we are not attached to England. Cornwall is a land on its own, divided by the Tamar from Devon, which is much gentler. Here we have quicksands pure gold in colour, a loneliness and a grandeur which are sometimes fearful to the stranger. It beckons or it seems too formidable, and the old laws still hold sway over the emotions of the Cornish people. The worst aspects of civilization haven't yet ruined our "elemental Tristan's land" as Lawrence called it.'

'Gard!' There was a note of vexation in Stella's voice. 'You never used to speak like this in the old days. What has got into you?'

'The devil that gets into the pilchard pie, perhaps.' He gave her a mocking look. 'The old days are over, Stella. A man with only one arm can't conduct symphonies, but with the help of some cowmen and a couple of tractors he can run a farm. It may not be a very romantic or glamorous occupation in your eyes, my dear, but it suits me.'

'You?' Her blue eyes took a languorous stroll over his dark features. 'You never could fool me, darling, and even if you can't conduct music, you could still compose it. Why don't you bother any more? Why have you buried yourself here in magnificent solitude?'

'The days of my magnificent solitude are over,' he drawled. 'That's why you were invited to the wilds, to meet my bride-to-be. It wasn't meant as a jest, Stella. The banns started to be called last week, and Ynis and I shall be married in a fortnight.'

The actress stared at him while a draught blew the candle-flames, and Ynis felt the duel play of the emotions between Gard and the cousin who had grown up with him, and been a part of him as, perhaps, no other woman could be. A strange love was at war between them, and looking at them across the table, proud-boned, cruel in speech at times, and gifted, she knew them to be two of a kind and meant by all the laws of Cornish blood to be together instead of held apart by his false engagement to herself.

She wanted to cry out to him to end the falseness and commit himself to what he truly wanted. Stella was akin to him. Her love like his could never be tender or patient and had a ruthless quality. They were well matched . . . as the sapphire had been matched to Stella's eyes.

Ynis wanted to wrench the ring off her hand . . . she wanted to fling it across the table, to rise and run from this house. The earlier rain had given rise to a moon and she would surely find her way to the station without walking into one of those golden quicksands which Gard had mentioned. Here at Sea Witch were the quicksands, pulling at her and holding her to a promise she felt certain she had never made. How could she have agreed to marry a man who showed not a spark of love for her? If she were the little upstart of Stella's description then she would surely take more delight in all those clothes he had given her, and in the ring which her right hand was crushing into the bones of her left hand. She wouldn't feel so strongly this sense of something being *wrong*.

When dinner came to an end they went to the drawing-room to drink their coffee. It was *café diable*. There were still some bottles of smuggled brandy in the cellar and Doom had fetched up a bottle so their coffee could be lit by the cognac.

'Napoleon,' Gard told Pierre. 'So you should enjoy it.'

'Undoubtedly, *m'sieur*. The British have always been as fond of stealing from us as we have been adept at stealing from them.'

'I wouldn't advise you to be too adept.' The flame licked blue across the surface of the coffee cup in Gard's hand, and it seemed to Ynis that a similar flame crept and curled in the depths of his eyes. As she sipped her own coffee, whose flame had been doused by the cream which Doom had poured, she found her eyes meeting the manservant's and she sensed once again that he knew all Gard's secrets, and had almost a diabolical loyalty towards him. He seemed to live and breathe with the permission of the man he served so efficiently, and with an air of having no one else but Gard to care about. He withdrew from the room as silently as if shod in velvet, and Stella gave a low trill of laughter.

'Your man Doom really is a treasure, Gard. He is the epitome of all stage butlers, whose devotion to his master is absolute and unquestioning. There isn't much he wouldn't do for you, is there?'

'He has been with me a good while and we are used to each other's ways.'

'Your right-hand man, Gard.' Stella said it deliberately and kept her eyes upon his face as she spoke. But his control was not to be shaken, and he stood there, his coffee cup in his hand, the saucer at rest on the black marble of the mantel, allowing Stella to look directly at the empty sleeve of his dinner jacket, pinned immaculately by the hand of Doom.

'I hope you've brought riding gear with you, Stella,' he said. 'A friend of mine has stables nearby and he has some splendid animals for hire. You were always fond of riding and I sometimes take my exercise that way . . . surprised that I still ride? My dear, I'm not so incapable that I can't manage a horse.'

'What about a woman?' she drawled, and there was a taunting, sensuous quality about her mouth, and about her figure as she sat there in a silk-tapestried chair and tilted her titian head in challenge, and invitation.

'You had best ask Ynis that question,' he rejoined.

The blue eyes narrowed, and then flashed a look at

Ynis, who sat on the edge of her chair and wished that Gard wouldn't use her as a weapon against Stella. She felt her own instinctive recoil from the scorn, and the glint of curiosity in Stella's eyes. 'I can't picture this little novice being all that hard to handle, Gard. She surely gives in to you without a struggle ... in fact I believe she's a little afraid of you. Can you have bullied her into becoming your fiancée? Or have you bribed her with the treasures of your house rather than the pleasures of your—'

'Stella!' His voice cracked across her words like a whiplash. 'You have never learned to be disciplined with your tongue or your emotions. You allow them to run away with you, as if life were a play and people were puppets, with no feelings to be hurt. I'm hardened by now against what you can say and do, but Ynis is young and vulnerable. She may take seriously some of the things you imply.'

'Are you afraid I might frighten her off before the wedding day?' Stella laughed, and the diamonds in her ear-lobes flashed against the red-gold fire of her lovely hair. 'I could certainly tell her a lot about you, Gard. She might not be aware that under the skin you and I are similar sort of people, with no patience with mediocrity, and about as easy to love as a pair of tigers. Does she love you?'

Ynis caught her breath, for it seemed incredible that anyone could be so audacious as to ask such a question. Her green eyes dwelt on his dark face, begging him to spare her, but it was Pierre who came to her rescue.

'You must show me the garden, *petite*, before the moon decides to go and hide itself. *M'sieur*, I have your permission?'

'Yes. Get yourself a wrap, Ynis. When the moon is bright it means a sea wind is blowing.'

She rose thankfully to her feet and felt desperately grateful to the Frenchman for making it possible for her to escape from this room, which had begun to feel like a cage in which a pair of tigers fought over her shrinking body. She hastened to the door, with Pierre following tall and lean behind her. They crossed the hall to the cloakroom, where she took a rain cloak off a hook. Pierre took it from her and placed it carefully about her shoulders, lifting the hood to cover her hair and to frame her rather white face.

'The eyes reveal what the lips would never dare to say,' he murmured. 'Another moment in there and you would have rushed from that room like a cornered hare. They are strong-willed, those two, eh? Elemental like this Cornwall to which Stella brings me with the excuse that I may find material here for a play. Ah yes, there is material for a drama, but I prefer comedy. Do we go this way?' He indicated a side door and she nodded and they went through into the moonlight and a soft gust of wind that blew the night scents of the flowers and creepers into their faces.

Ynis took a deep breath of the fresh air, dispelling from her nostrils the expensive perfume which had clung to the velvet folds of Stella's gown.

They walked silently for a while, along the path that

95

circled the lawns to the stone balcony overlooking the sea. Ynis often came here alone, and by the light of the moon she could make out the sets of initials carved into the stone. She knew exactly the place where the initials GSC were crossed by an arrow in the shape of an S. Here they would have stood, the sea wind blowing that Borgia red hair into a glowing tangle about the wilful face of Stella, whose eyes would have watched avidly as the point of the knife scarred the stone with Gard's youthful declaration of love.

Her image and her cruelty had scarred his heart in the same manner, and the thought of marrying him was for Ynis as cold as the sea below the wall where she stood with Pierre Dumont.

His back was to the parapet and he was studying the peaked roofs and towers of Sea Witch, and the wind-blown elms like witches themselves. 'It is a strange house,' he said quietly. 'Not at all beautiful on the outside, but he has put much beauty inside it. I think that Gard St. Clair is rather like his house, a strange mixture of a man. Perhaps more dangerous than Stella, who says things for their effect without always meaning them.'

'If you are referring to Gard's remark at dinner, then please forget it. I am sure he would never kill for me.' Ynis shot a smile at Pierre. 'He isn't at all in love with me. He only wanted to show Stella that he doesn't spend his time down here in Cornwall brooding over her triumphs in London. I came along . . . I was useful for his purpose. The farce won't go as far as a marriage.'

'Are you entirely sure of that?' A match flared and Pierre lit a Gauloise and puffed smoke at the moon. The aroma clung in the air along with his question, and Ynis could feel him studying her profile, and treating her as an adult rather than the half-child whom Gard had control of; whom Gard had known as homeless and poor. For Pierre she had the quality of an enigma, dressed in lacy white and silver shoes, with a pearl hung in a strand of gold about her neck. She bore the semblance of a girl who was cared for, and so it must look as if she lied when she told this man that Gard felt nothing for her but a sense of responsibility because she was alone in the world.

'Gard must always have loved Stella,' she said. 'Look, here are their initials carved long ago, when they were boy and girl together.'

'Boys become men and the old loves change and take new shapes. You wear his ring,' Pierre touched her cold, ringed hand as it lay on the cold stone, the sapphire gleaming in the moonlight that broke the ocean into countless silver ripples. 'You became his fiancée, so you must feel something for him.'

'You heard what Stella said about me. I am a little upstart who is greedy for the good things he can provide. I have never lived in a big house like this one, nor have I worn fine clothes before.' Her eyes looked immense as they dwelt on the face of the man beside her, the outward corners of them slanting like a faun's. 'It could all be true, for I can't remember why I agreed to

97

marry him. I had concussion and it has played odd tricks with my memory. I know that Gard was never a complete stranger to me, but I also sense that he was never close to me. By some odd chance we met, and that is all I know for sure. The rest is a blank. The car that knocked me down cut off the past for me.'

'As that car in Oxford Street was instrumental in cutting off Gard's right arm.'

Shock registered in her eyes. 'I – I didn't know that it happened in a car accident. Gard never speaks of it, and the servants are forbidden to mention a word relating to it.'

'You mean to tell me that you have no knowledge of what happened to maim him?' Pierre looked amazed. 'Would you like me to tell you about that day?'

'No – yes,' she sighed. 'I must know, and yet I dread knowing. I wonder, Pierre. Could I have been involved, in some obscure way?'

'I doubt it, *petite*.' He touched her cheek very gently. 'You would have been a mere schoolgirl, being taught by the nuns, and I am sure a very good girl. It happened five years ago, at the height of his fame, and when the flame burned hot and bright between him and Stella. You wish to hear?'

'I have no other choice, Pierre.'

CHAPTER SIX

Ynis had let back the hood of her rain cloak and she welcomed the feel of the breeze as it rose off the sea and combed the hair from her brow. She felt tense and half afraid of what she was about to hear. She waited as Pierre Dumont took a final pull at his cigarette and then tossed the stub down towards the sea. The silent seconds passed as the moon sailed through the sky and the stars swam in its orbit like a shoal of glittering fish.

It was a beautiful night, quivering with scents and soft country sounds. It was a night meant for the revelation of love instead of the relating of a tragedy, and a tremor of emotion ran through Ynis as her companion began to speak.

'Gard St. Clair lived in London at that time, in a smart apartment near the Albert Hall. I once saw him conduct there Verdi's Requiem, and I was very much moved. In his hand the baton was a wand of magic and musical inspiration, there was no doubt of it. He's a Doctor of Music, of course, and he could also play the organ superbly – especially Bach. I have several of his recordings – see you, how could he help but become a different man from the famed man that he was? How can he always control his bitterness?'

Pierre was looking at Ynis, he seemed to hesitate,

and then he murmured: ' "Be brave and patient, swiftly shall pass thy night of trial here." Those are the closing words of *The Dream of Gerontius*. That man Gard, he also had his dreams, but now, alas, he seems as cold as a wine cellar, with all the richness of him bottled up, sealed off, buried among the cobwebs of his dreams. This is the man whom you know – it was another whom Stella knew. She was there at Covent Garden, the night before that terrible thing happened to him. She was in his private box to watch him conduct with all his compelling power a gala ballet performance. An exciting night in that most exciting theatre, with its red seats, its many lights, and the spell of the dance. Gislova was on stage, being partnered by Anton Loder. These names are no doubt strange to you, but these people were friends of Stella and Gard. They were part of their working world and their playtime.

'Then, within a matter of hours, all this fame and glamour was shattered for him, and the dreams became a nightmare. He was in Oxford Street on some errand, and like others beguiled by all those shops he was strolling along in the spring sunshine, feeling good with himself, satisfied with his work of the night before, with the music, perhaps, still in his head. All at once there was a screaming of brakes, and shouts of alarm as a large car ran amok and suddenly mounted the pavement near where Gard was walking. He and two other people were flung off their feet by the momentum of the crazy car, carried on the bonnet for several yards and thrust like objects through the plate-glass windows of a store. It was a very terrible thing to happen, and it happened so swiftly, in a matter of seconds. A woman was killed, another was badly lacerated ... and the right arm of Gard St. Clair, the conductor of music, was literally severed by the razor edge of the glass as it broke under the impact of the car.'

Pierre drew a deep sigh and fell silent as he allowed Ynis to absorb the shock of his words ... and they were shocking, evoking a picture so agonizing that she cried out. 'Oh no! Not like that ... so cruelly, with the sun still shining!'

'Exactly like that,' Pierre said, inexorably. 'But that was not all the horror. While he lay bereft, with the onlookers crowding round, he was robbed of his wallet. He felt the fingers of the swine sliding from his pocket, and he saw the face of the man a moment before he passed out. At the hospital, not knowing who he was because his wallet was gone and his means of identification, they amputated the arm to save his life. His right arm that was his life, more or less. Later the wallet was found in the gutter some yards from where the accident occurred and, of course, all the money was gone, but his address was there, stamped into the leather. He was identified, but it was too late by then for a miraculous surgeon like his friend Sir Henry Coburn to go to work on that arm, which his skill might have saved. The arm was gone, and Gard's career was gone with it. In time his body recovered, but it seems that the best part of his heart was incinerated with the muscles and the supple wrist and the fingers of his right arm. What is a conductor without a right arm? He is like a racehorse without a right leg.'

The sea and the moon were queerly shimmering in front of Ynis's eyes, and when she looked at Pierre there were tears in her eyes. 'Poor man! To live always with the knowledge that his arm might have been saved if that little rat had not robbed him! How unbearable for him!'

'Pickpockets are quite without conscience or scruple, *petite*. Of honour they know nothing, and care even less. There on the pavement, perhaps to die and never to know, lay this well-dressed man, quite obviously a gentleman and with money, in his pocket. The hands of a thief are sly and quick, and the action is accomplished in almost the wink of an eye. Yet how it must have shaken even that *mauvais type* to see upon him the open eyes of his victim, aware of what was happening even if pain and shock had robbed him of the power of speech. It was thirty pounds that were stolen, along with a brilliant career. Again was Judas tempted by thirty pieces of silver!'

Ynis listened to the low down crooning of the sea ... or did it sob as it washed against the rocks of Barbizon, dark shapes along the shore? 'I can't understand how Stella could let him down after what happened to him. If she loved him, how could she add cruelty to his suffering? How can she come here and pretend that she still cares for him?'

'She is a devil-angel, that one.' A note of cynicism

mingled with the respect of one professional for another; of a playwright for an actress of consummate skill who made his plays a dazzling success on the stages of London, New York and Paris. 'She likes to keep enslaved the men she has stooped to love. In her way, which would be different from your way, *petite*, she loves St. Clair, but after the accident, after some private bitterness between them, he refused to live her life, and she will never live far from the bright lights of the theatre; from the challenge of being and remaining a star. The pride and wilfulness they share is in their blood, for they are second cousins, and Stella's own middle name is St. Clair. This is what binds them, and at the same time keeps them separated. If that awful thing had never happened to him that morning in Oxford Street, then they would have married, a pair of stars in orbit, but Gard will never be a satellite of his wife. Not only has he the head and the face of a gothic martyr, but I think he has the strength to deny himself, to resist Stella rather than risk what he has found here in Cornwall with you, Ynis.'

'And what do you imagine he has found with me?' It was her turn to sound a little cynical. 'What do I know of music and the world that meant so much to him? What do I know about managing a man at all, let alone one like Gard St. Clair? You have told me his story and made me feel sorry for him . . . but pity is the last thing he wants from anyone! It's Stella whom he needs, not a little nobody like me!'

'*Assez de tout ça!*' Pierre gripped her by the shoulders, and then framed her face with his hands, tilting it to the moon so he could look into her eyes. 'You have the advantage of being innocent, you with your half-moon of a face and your jade eyes. You have never been guilty of hurting him, and I believe Stella did so after the accident. She may have revealed her horror of disfigurement, and he would have been terribly sensitive at that time. The trouble with actresses is that they are instinctive mirrors of all the emotions, and Gard would have been quick to notice the smallest retreat from his mutilation. How ironical of the gods to take not his left arm but his right one! It meant that all he had trained for, and been acclaimed for, was ended, and that not only was he disfigured, he was out of work! When he left the hospital he left London and he travelled abroad for about a year. Then he came home to Cornwall and there was no more talk of a marriage between him and Stella.'

Ynis stood there between the hands of Pierre, outwardly quiet, yet inwardly so disturbed that she was almost angry with him for telling her about Gard and making her see him as a human being who could bleed instead of feel like stone.

'The strong are often vulnerable because their wounds are often deep,' said Pierre. 'He needs you—'

'But most of all,' she cried, 'he needed to let Stella know that he had found a girl to take her place. He telephoned the news to her!'

'I believe she telephoned him, *petite*. A rumour was

circulating at her favourite dress houses that Gard St. Clair was buying clothes for a young woman – everything, so it was obviously a trousseau. I am quite sure that she invited herself to Sea Witch, and no doubt the devil in him invited her to meet his bride-to-be. Can't you understand?'

'Not really, Pierre. I'm not worldly enough to take in my stride the fact that I'm expected to marry a man who all his life has loved another woman! To see them together is to realize how well matched they are, both of them so clever, and as careless of being cruel as a tiger that stretches its claws and draws blood almost without knowing it. They were brought up to be aware of their brilliance and to be arrogantly sure of themselves. Both of them ... they make me feel so insignificant. I bet at this moment she is laughing at him for even proposing that a girl like me should be his bride. She knows, as I know, that he is playing a game with the pair of us!'

Pierre stared down at her, raking his eyes over the white pleading of her face, the cry for help on her lips. She was afraid, and bewildered by her own fears and compassions. They had mixed together, these adverse emotions, until she had to cry out to someone to help her.

'La pauvre.' He was too Gallic, too emotional himself not to be moved by her plea, and he pulled her into his arms and held her close to him, there in the moonlight, his hand moving over the soft, unevenly cut surface of her hair. She could hear him murmuring words in French, and the strange thing was she understood them. How could that be? Had one of the nuns at the convent been a Frenchwoman who had taught her the language? She was so amazed by this new discovery about herself that it came as a complete shock when someone broke in harshly, in English, upon the Gallic murmur of Pierre's voice.

'What the devil are you playing at? I warned you, Dumont, that I wouldn't tolerate a flirtation with this girl! Take your hands off her – stroking and pawing her as if she were one of your little stage girls after a part in one of your plays!'

Angry, insolent words that drove every particle of colour from Pierre's face as he let go of Ynis and stared at the dark, towering figure of Gard, the sea-dark skin drawn tightly over the harsh features, the black brows joined solidly above the glittering eyes. He looked as if he could kill, but Pierre stood his ground, and of the two he seemed less foreign in that moment, less at the mercy of a quick and arrogant temper.

'Don't be so quick to insult your fiancée, *m'sieur*,' he flung at Gard. 'You can't know her very well if you think she would play games with me behind your back. She needs friendship, this one, not an affair.'

'A close friendship, from the look of it,' Gard retorted. 'Do you always embrace your friends and whisper sweet French nothings in their ears? I should imagine it must be a trifle embarrassing for the men of your acquaintance.'

'Gard, stop it!' Ynis was suddenly tired of it all, of

being the target between him and Stella, and now Pierre. *Her* feelings seemed to count for nothing; she was the little nobody who must be grateful for being here at all. Here, in this house, where the old emotions were running riot tonight and putting a strain on all their nerves. She would leave in the morning, quietly and early, and hope he would find some way to be happy with Stella.

'I'm tired,' she said. 'I'm going to bed.' She ran past Gard towards the house, taking the quick way across the grass and feeling the moisture spattering against her ankles. The folds of the cloak flew out behind her, and the moonlight gave to her fleeing figure a poignancy that held the two men immobile until she was out of sight. She entered her suite through the terrace windows and she drew the curtains close behind her, shutting out the moon that sailed so serenely above the chimneys of Sea Witch.

The tiredness spread all through her body, making her feel cold, and she knelt on the tiger rug and turned on the electric fire; for a long, long time she gazed at the glow and felt again that tingling pity and horror for Gard . . . but all the same she must leave him. She must beware of pity, for he demanded more than that of her. Only by leaving Sea Witch could she be sure that he didn't use her as the ultimate weapon against Stella. Only by leaving them together could she hope to keep them together.

She drew the sapphire from her finger and took it to the dressing-table where she carefully placed it on the crystal ring-guard. It gleamed like a cold blue eye as she raised her hands and unclasped the chain and pearl which Gard had given her to wear. It lay like a frozen teardrop in the palm of her hand . . . there was indeed a superstition about pearls, and tonight she had learned how tears could hurt.

It was late when she heard the closing of doors along the corridor, and later still before she slept, but restlessly, troubled by her dreams. It was dark, the moon shut out by the drawn curtains, when a sound of some sort awoke her and she lay in the darkness listening to the soft ticking of the clock, waiting tensely for the sound to come again so that she might identify it.

Ah . . . she half sat up and the covers fell from her shoulders. It was out there on the terrace, a footfall in the silence of the night, so close to her french window that her heart began to hammer and she pictured a prowler out there, seeking a way into the house in search of valuables. At once her hand shot towards the bedside lamp, for a sudden light might scare him off, but in the darkness she misjudged the distance to the lamp and sent it toppling over. It made a thump on the table top that sounded in the quiet like a drum-beat. She caught her breath and could almost hear the prowler breathing outside her window . . . then her heart seemed to kick her breast as she heard the click of the catch and saw the curtains swing open in the moonlight that lay opal-pale along the terrace. A man stepped into her bedroom!

'Don't scream,' he said, 'or throw anything. I heard

you knock something over, so I knew you were awake.'

'You!' The deep, almost throaty tones were unmistakable, and so was the height of the intruder. The curtains fell into place again, and her hands shook with an even greater nervousness as she righted the lamp and plunged the switch. The gold-shaded light revealed him, framed tall and dark against the golden sweep of the curtains. His black hair was ruffled and he wore a dark robe with the right sleeve hanging loose at his side. He blinked at the light, like a great cat coming in out of the night.

'What do you want, Gard?' She clutched the bed-cover against her, but she knew that his eyes had seen the pale slimness of her bare shoulders, from which the pink straps of her nightdress had slipped, as silk slips on silky skin.

'I – I don't really know.' He thrust a hand across his hair and sat down on the foot of her bed. 'I suppose my pacing aroused you – did you take me for a thief out there?'

'Yes.' She stared at the strangeness of him in her bedroom at night. It had never seemed significant that he should be here during the day, but the glow of the bedside lamp and the little heap of discarded underwear, which she had been too lazy to fold neatly on the dressing stool, added a sense of intimacy that was truly alarming. She felt him looking closely at her, and her own gaze slid from object to object in the room, avoiding his dark-robed figure and the glimpse of black hair in the neck opening of his pyjamas. The ruffled look of him suggested that he had been to bed but had arisen a short while ago to pace restlessly the stone pavement of the terrace.

'I hate tossing and turning,' he said. 'I couldn't sleep, so I tried pacing myself tired. I'm sorry I disturbed you, and gave you a bit of a scare. I must say you look pretty white — would you like a drink of water?'

'I'm all right — I'm not about to faint,' she retorted, and she was annoyed with him because he made her feel more nervous than a burglar would have done. 'You are funny, Gard. One moment you think I'm brazen, and the next that I'm spiritless. I'm *me*, Ynis Raiford, and I can't be moulded like Galatea into something that would please you better. The only woman who will ever make you feel truly alive is Stella, and one or the other of you is going to have to submit—'

'It will never be me!' He leaned towards Ynis and his eyes were burning with the dark memory of pain; harsh lines clawed his face and outlined the boldness of his mouth. She felt again the intense masculinity of him, and all the suppressed passion of the past five years. 'Yes, I have my soul scars and they will always be a part of me, but I'm done with the old dreams and I want new ones. I want you, my solemn child, and I shall have you. You owe me yourself, do you know that?'

'Y-you mean I am in your debt?' She could feel the

weight of him against her legs, and the inadequate shield of the bedcovers, and how easy it would be for him to master her frailty with his strength. She had only words for weapons, and even those he could twist and bend to his own purpose. 'Am I being asked to pay for the clothes in that cupboard over there, and for the nursing you provided for me, not to mention a roof over my head? Are you sure you'll be getting value for your money? I know nothing of men, and even less about handling servants and running a house like Sea Witch. I'm a joke above and below stairs. Even Alice the maid has more *savoir faire* than I have.'

'Alice has abominable taste in music,' he drawled. 'And I don't doubt that her sex education has already begun. With you, my pet, I start almost from scratch, and I am arrogant enough to like the idea of creating my own woman from a bare little rib.' His eyes dwelt on the bedcovers which she held against her, and a mocking little smile flickered in his eyes. 'The attitude you are adopting at present is far more inciting than actually seeing you in your nightdress. You actually look as if you expect me to ravish you, and quite frankly it might be the easiest way of getting you to the altar. You might not make such a struggle of it if I compromised you here and now.'

'Y-you wouldn't dare!' The colour flamed in her cheeks, and she sat there in the great bed rigid with fear of him. 'You wouldn't be such a cad!'

'What an old-fashioned word for it, my pet.' He sprawled closer to her, a dark tiger of a man, a black pelt of hair across his chest, and a dangerous tumult in his blood from his long denial of Stella, whom he had loved as a boy and as a man. It was Stella who had made him restless tonight; his withheld longing for her which had made him toss and turn in his bed. He had to torment in his turn, and Ynis was at hand, within reach, and inhibited by her natural shyness and her convent upbringing so that screaming would somehow be more shaming than anything he might do. His eyes knew, tauntingly, that she wouldn't scream and bring Stella on the scene.

'Cads are the men who don't offer marriage, before or after the event,' he drawled, and before she could stop him he had taken hold of her left hand and was looking at it. 'I see you don't wear your ring in bed.'

'It isn't my ring – it isn't, and I don't care if you break my hand for saying it!' Her green eyes blazed defiance at him, and her left shoulder was bare, fingered by the gold shadowing of the lamp on the left side of the bed. The silk coverlet slid down, and his eyes followed the movement to her young breast under the pink chiffon silk. The lids of his eyes seemed to grow heavy and the lashes thickened with shadow.

'Why do you insist that the ring isn't yours when I gave it to you?' His voice held the deep crushiness of velvet, but hidden there was an undertone of threat. He was daring her to tell him why she hated the ring, and at the same time he was warning her that the leash on his self-control was fast slipping. Ynis knew that she could still placate him if she wished, but if she went on stripping to the bones the truth of their relationship he would let slip his restraint altogether and a far more shattering truth would be hers in the morning.

She would have to marry him!

She stared at him and her heart jolted, and her gaze sprang to the tiger head that snarled in front of the fireplace. She heard him laugh, softly and knowingly.

'Is that how you think of me?' he drawled, and her hand was turned within his and she felt lips against her wrist, at the exact place where her pulse throbbed. She started as if a flame had brushed her skin, but when she would have pulled free of his fingers they tightened and they pulled until with a little gasp she felt herself toppling forward against him. His arm adroitly gripped her around the waist and she was beneath him, there on the bed, and his lips were only inches from hers, and a diabolical little smile glimmered in his eyes as they looked down into hers.

'You are right, my sweet, gentle, innocent child. The ring was meant for Stella; as you noticed, the sapphire exactly matches her eyes. I ordered it for her the morning after we decided to be married, in London five years ago. By the time it was sent to me, Stella and I were no longer on the threshold of marriage, and I let you wear the ring, my pet, because I wanted to see pain in her sapphire eyes. You shudder, Ynis! You don't like cruelty, do you? You believe in goodness and mercy, as you should, little one, with your upbringing. I used to believe in those virtues myself, as a young idealistic boy, and even as a man, but I lost them . . . I lost many things, but you I intend to have!'

His lips came down on hers as he finished speaking, and there seemed nothing else alive in the world but Gard's mouth, seeking her, finding her, and not caring that she fought him until her strength was as crushed as her lips and her young, slim, frightened body.

She couldn't scream . . . but suddenly, and shockingly, someone did cry out, there by the door. Everything went still . . . the lips holding hers were as if turned to stone. Then Gard raised himself and turned his head in the direction of that choked cry. His black hair was unruly from the desperately wild hands of Ynis, and all the smouldering drowsiness had gone from his eyes and they were alert as a cat's.

'Stella!'

Even as the name escaped him, Ynis whipped her head up and she saw the swirl of a Chinese robe, a peacock-coloured sleeve, and she winced as the door slammed behind the actress. The silence then was that of two people who were bereft of words, then Gard let go of her and he slid from the bed. With the deliberateness of a man who was searching for the graphic words he smoothed his hair with his hand.

'Caught out, they call it,' he said, and there was a twist to his lip. 'Stella always had an inquisitive streak and I might have guessed that she would have to find out if I was calling on you ahead of the nuptials. Now she knows, doesn't she?'

'You meant her to know,' Ynis flared, and so white

was her face that her eyes were emerald, sharp-pointed against the pallor of her skin. 'Don't pretend to me that you've ever forgotten a thing relating to Stella. You know her as you know yourself, and you made sure she heard you out on the terrace, as I did. You timed the whole thing perfectly. You wanted her to find me in your arms, so compromised that I should have to marry you and provide a shield against the weak spot in your armour, Gard. The weak spot directly where your heart is! Stella's in your heart, and in your blood, and I won't be used to keep her at a distance. I – I have my pride, you know!'

'And what will your pride be worth, Ynis, when it gets around that you have been my mistress?'

'But I haven't—'

'Do you imagine, my ingenuous child, that Stella thought we were merely rehearsing just now?' Abruptly he leaned forward and adjusted the pink silk which his lips had disarranged. His fingertips were like points of fire against the softly supple skin of her young breast. And hating him, despising his touch, she struck away his hand. His lips thinned and his eyelids narrowed across the darkness of his eyes.

'Very well,' he crisped, 'shall I throw you out of my house in the morning, like a used creature?'

'Do what you like,' she spat furiously at him. 'I'd sooner be anything but your wife. Anything! Scrubbing kitchen floors would be preferable to being made love to by a—' She broke off; he was a devil, but he wasn't quite a brute, and she bit back the word before

115

she spoke it.

'A cripple, were you going to say?' The words leapt at her, quick as her own but even more cruel. 'Were you going to call me that to my face? Even Stella didn't actually say the word, she only looked it.'

'Gard—'

But he was turning away, he was leaving her bedroom, pausing a moment by the dressing-table to take the sapphire ring from the ring-guard. He studied it a moment and then slipped it into the pocket of his robe.

'Good night,' he said, in a remote voice. 'We can't discuss the future in our present mood. We will leave things as they are until tomorrow.'

The door closed behind him, yet his tall, dark impression seemed to remain, and his voice seemed to leave the echo of his awful words. 'A cripple – were you about to call me that to my face?'

Ynis huddled down into the dishevelled bedcovers, and she pressed her hands over her ears in almost a childish defence against the words that reverberated in her mind.

She had never dreamed of calling Gard such a thing, but he had gone from her bedroom believing that she shrank from him because he had lost his arm . . . lost it so cruelly in the sunlight of a spring day, in the shambles of cruel broken glass. She wanted with all her being to go and protest to him that his amputation did not repel her . . . but if she did so she would be closing the door on her deeper need to escape from Sea Witch.

From a situation which marriage to him could never resolve.

Neither at night nor during the day would she be able to dismiss from her thoughts or her feelings the love for Stella that was deep in his bones.

Therein lay her rejection of his embraces ... whenever he touched her or put his lips to hers, he would be thinking of Stella. He would be desiring her perfect body, her knowing lips, her whispers that would always hold the memories they had shared in their youth and in their fame.

A coldness crept through Ynis and she slid down into her bed and felt herself trembling with the reaction of the assault on her emotions. Her lips still seemed to burn from Gard's savage kisses; her body ached from being forced to yield to him ... she didn't dare to think of how far he would have gone if Stella had not intruded upon them.

She hid her face in her pillow, feeling the skin burning against the coolness of the linen. She longed desperately for the morning to come; she wouldn't have to face Gard or Stella, for she would leave Sea Witch as early as possible. She no longer had the ring to pawn, but he had left the pearl and chain, and it would fetch enough to pay her fare to London.

Once in the great city she would be anonymous, and there she could approach a convent community for help.

CHAPTER SEVEN

SHE had planned to wake so early, but her exhausted emotions played a trick on her and sunlight was flooding into her room and Alice was at her bedside with a breakfast tray when she stirred awake.

'Oh . . .' She stared up at Alice. 'What time is it?'

'Just gone ten, miss. We were given orders not to disturb you.' There seemed to be an insinuating note in the girl's voice, and her eyes wandered with curiosity over the disarray of Ynis's bed. 'You must have had a restless night, miss. You're usually such a tidy sleeper and an early riser. Up with the lark usually, aren't you?'

'Yes.' Ynis snapped the word, for she was annoyed with herself for oversleeping today of all days, and she didn't like the way Alice was regarding her. 'I'll have breakfast by the window, so please put the tray on the table there.'

'As you wish, Miss Ynis.' The note of authority was unusual in the quiet, almost shy voice, and Alice widened her eyes a moment before she turned from the bed and obeyed the order. Ynis slipped out of bed and into her robe, and in order to avoid any more conversation with Alice she went into the bathroom. When she came out again the young maid was gone, and the sunlight was gleaming on the coffee pot and the plate covers, there by the window. She sat down at the small table and poured herself a cup of coffee, and as she sipped it she stared across the wall of the terrace and heard the carefree sound of the birds in the shrubberies.

Everything seemed quiet but for the birds. There was no sign of Stella or the two men, and she wished now that she had asked Alice if they had gone riding or swimming. Like Gard, Stella had been brought up on this coastline, so she would have no fear of the rather wild sea off Barbizon. She would look marvellous in a bathing suit, but Gard wouldn't swim with her. Ynis knew it instinctively. He would always swim alone, for his stroke would be ungainly, one-sided, and too stark a reminder that he couldn't match the perfection of Stella's body.

Ynis forced herself to eat her breakfast, for it might be some hours before she tasted food again, and she was determined to leave Sea Witch today. In her youth and her inexperience she couldn't cope with a man who made the demands of a lover without *loving* her.

By ten-thirty Ynis was wearing slacks and a pale yellow sweater, with a suède jacket whose collar was lined with velvet. In her pocket was the pearl trinket which must pay her fare to London, and after a last look round her bedroom she hastened through the terrace doors, away from the memory of last night . . . the angry words . . . the savage kisses . . . the conflict she could no longer face.

She went along the terrace, hurrying away, wanting

no part of unholy wedlock.

It was a morning filled with the promise of a fine day, and the air was filled refreshingly with the scents of moorland and sea. Aware that she might be seen by the staff if she kept to this side of the house, she made her way to the west side, where the rather unkempt drive led down to the road.

When she reached the gates she turned for a final look at the house, old and mullioned from this angle, with slender towers rising to peaks like the hats of witches. In daylight Sea Witch was less mysterious than at sunset, when the latticed windows glowed like rubies, and the ravens came in from the moors and settled on the chimneys to croak at the sky.

Gard had once invited her into the west wing, but she had never gone there with him. She wondered why as she stood by the gates, with her hand poised to push them open.

He had said that there she would remember what he had been to her . . . now, as she left him, she realized how deeply she had feared to remember if hate or love had driven her away from him that night she had been hurt in the rain.

Never for a moment had she been truly a part of Sea Witch, and she would soon be forgotten by those who really belonged to this house. She would be the one to remember . . . a fleeting hour now and then when a sort of happiness had been hers . . . clutched at, child-like, when she explored an old abandoned boat at the end of the bay, or ate cold grouse sandwiches with

Gard the night he came in late from the barns.

The gate groaned shut behind her and the road lay sunlit ahead of her, as if this time there would be nothing to hinder her from getting away from the house she had half grown to love.

The road sloped up and down to take the undulations of the moors, and the beguiling scent of gorse blew across those wild fields, holding a sort of bitter honey that tingled in her nostrils and made her head rear back to take the sun and the scent into her very skin. She passed moor cottages, with roughstone walls, sloping roofs and deeply indented windows and doorways. They stood there amidst the little skull-cap flowers and the turf as if they also grew from the earth; there was washing blowing on a line beside one of these houses, and there was a naturalness about it, a sense of home and comfort that made Ynis feel terribly alone.

If only such a house was hers, but she was on her way to London, where the houses were filled with strangers, and the streets teemed with traffic which filled the air with the fumes of exhaust.

There you couldn't smell the gorse, or hear the seagulls as they flew in from the rocks of Barbizon. She paused on the breast of the road and stared across the moors, and she had a sudden longing to walk there before she reached the village. In the distance she could see a tall moorland stone; she would walk just so far and fill her lungs with the wonderful air, and perhaps touch the standing stone for luck. Her blood leapt and her feet seemed lighter as she ran down the sloping green verge into the tall ragged grass.

A bird flew out from its hiding place and startled her, and then she laughed at her own nervousness and felt the spring of the grass about her trousered legs as she walked towards the tall, dark stone that was left there from the pagan rites of long ago, where strange cults had held their meetings, and where strange whispers from the past might linger. At nightfall she might have hesitated to approach the stone, but in daylight it was merely a boundary she had set herself; it represented her final good-bye to Barbizon, a gesture to the old gods of the moors that they make her journey a safe one.

She came to it at last and it stood there deep in the ground, smoothed by the weather to almost the shine of basalt, and it was shaped like a chair. A Druid's chair, she thought, touching the stone with her hand and closing her eyes to make her pagan wish. *Let me find a place somewhere, a place to which I can belong. Let Sea Witch fade from my mind like a dream.*

But in that instant what she heard was like a scream out of a nightmare ... it rose up from the hollowed ground only a short distance from the stone, and when she ran to look downwards the blood ran cold in her veins. A young horse was tossing and writhing in the bright green mire of a moorland bog, the gleam of sweat on its neck as it struggled to pull itself out of the wide sucking mouth of the death hole. Again it screamed and its rolling eyes seemed to look at Ynis for a maddened moment, as if in appeal for help.

She must fetch help, instantly, and she fled back across the tangled grass and the gorse to the road, panting for breath as she clambered up the incline. The stone cottage she had passed was about a quarter of a mile back down the road and she hoped as she made for it that there would be someone on the premises who could bring help to that poor animal before it was choked by the green mud.

The image of the animal's terrified struggle was stark in her mind, erasing all other thoughts as she sped as fast as her feet could carry her in the direction of the cottage. Even as she glimpsed that flapping line of washing, she caught the sound of a car on the road behind her. She whirled to look, and then ran half-way into the road to wave it to a halt. As the brakes squealed and the car stopped, the head of the driver was thrust out of the open window. '*Parbleu!*' he exclaimed. 'The crazy child is Ynis!'

The door at the other side of the car was thrust open and a tall figure emerged. 'Ynis – it is you!'

The man confronting her on the road was Gard St. Clair, and the strange thing was that she felt only a rush of thankfulness. She rushed to him and caught at his arm. 'There's a horse trapped on the moor in a bog hole!' she told him breathlessly. 'I was going to that house to get help – you must do something! The poor thing is crazed—'

He stared down at her, raking his eyes over her anxious face. 'How long ago did you see this?' he demanded.

123

'About seven or eight minutes. I've been running as fast as I could — Gard, please do something!' She shook his arm urgently. 'Don't just stand there, or the animal will die!'

He cast a glance across the moors and she heard him give a sigh. 'We would be too late, Ynis. The poor beast's struggles will have pulled him all the way in by now. I'm sorry, child—'

'Oh, don't be sorry!' She let go of him, but as she turned to dash in the direction of the cottage, his hand checked her, painfully and forcibly.

'I tell you it's no use. I've known these bogs for years, and a tractor and ropes would be needed, fast, to pull a horse out of one of them. It's over by now, Ynis. The animal's misery is ended.'

She shuddered and knew he must be right, but she felt driven to argue with him, even as Pierre climbed out of the car and joined them. 'You're always certain of things,' she shouted at Gard. 'You always know better than anyone else what should be done, or left undone. You think yourself infallible — but I think you're as hard as one of those stones that stand on the moors!'

'What is all this?' asked Pierre. 'What has happened?'

'Ynis has just seen a horse dragged into a bog.' Gard spoke the words gravely. 'I've seen it happen before to the ponies that run wild on the moors—'

'This wasn't a wild pony,' she broke in, and now she was trembling from the reaction of seeing an animal die in terror. Her eyes raised to Gard's face were mirrors of that recent awful scene. 'I could just see the reins around its throat . . . don't you understand, it was a saddle horse, Gard, and so it had a rider! There was no sign of the rider . . . whoever it was might have fallen into the bog as well!'

'*Mon Dieu!*' Pierre's face went pale. 'Was the horse a chestnut?'

'Yes.' How could she ever forget the sweat streaming down that dark red neck, and the splashes of sedge against the coppery coat of the poor beast? 'Without any doubt he was a chestnut.'

'My God!' Gard's features seemed to stand out like iron under the taut skin of his face. 'Come, Ynis, into the car! Dumont, we must drive back at once to the stables. That mount could be Stella's!'

They hastened to the car, and Ynis could feel her legs shaking as she climbed into the back seat while Gard again took the seat next to Pierre. The morning which had started with sunshine was turning grey as clouds cobbled the sky. Ynis stared at the black peak of hair stabbing the nape of Gard's neck. As Pierre took the wheel and swung the car about, she heard him say: 'It will be terrible if so shocking a thing has happened to her, who so loved everything to be bright and gay. *Tragique!*'

Gard made no answer and it seemed to Ynis that he was stunned and facing the awful fact that he might have lost Stella completely, with no hope of ever seeing that vivacious face again, or hearing that honeyed slightly malicious voice, with its undertones of seductive laughter.

Abruptly he turned in his seat to face Ynis. 'You saw nothing at the scene but the horse? No fallen glove or scarf? No sign that a woman had been there? Think, Ynis! Go over it in your mind—'

'I can't get it out of my mind,' she retorted, and she was clenching her hands in her lap in an attempt to control her shaken nerves; digging her fingernails into her palms until her fingers ached. 'The horse was screaming and rolling its eyes and trying so desperately hard to pull itself out of the mud. That was all I was aware of . . . even when I noticed the reins, it was because they seemed to be strangling the poor creature. It was awful, seeing him and not being able to do a thing to help.'

'I know.' His eyes seemed to stab deep into hers, sending a strange shock right through her. She had not escaped after all. That strange web of circumstance still held her captive, as his dark eyes held her and wouldn't let go until he had, it seemed, searched her very soul.

'You were taking a walk on the moors, eh?'

'The sun was shining—' She shivered, for now the sun had quite gone in behind the clouds and she felt as if she hated the moors for their remorselessness. 'Why did Stella go riding alone? Did you have words with her, Gard?'

'She wanted to ride alone, that's all, so Pierre drove her to the stables and then he took me to the village so I could pick up a small package from the postmistress there. Stella's an excellent horsewoman, and she knows the moors, but we both heard her ask Dick Travis for a chestnut horse. She laughed, in that way of hers, and said that a red mount would suit her colouring and her mood—' He broke off, frowning and dragging his bottom lip under the bite of his strong teeth. It was the first sign he had given of his racked emotions ... of having let his game of revenge get out of hand. He knew very well that Stella in a mood would not be gentle with a horse, for last night he had aroused her jealousy ... shown her deliberately that he would desire someone else.

The speeding car made an abrupt left turn on to a dirt track between a couple of white posts. A long stone house came into view, and when they halted at the side of it, the row of stables could be seen through an archway, gabled and set with a sundial. There was a clatter of hooves as a party of riders came single file under the archway. As they passed the car they turned to glance at the three people emerging from it.

One of them called a greeting to Gard, but he seemed not to hear and he strode ahead of Ynis and Pierre into the stable yard. 'Dick!' he called out. 'Where are you, man?'

'The poor devil is very anxious.' Pierre held Ynis by the elbow and looked down at her. 'You must find all this very painful yourself? You are at the centre of the drama, are you not?'

'I seem to be the whip which those two use to strike at each other.' She drew a shaky breath. 'Why is love such a complicated business? It should be so simple and natural, shouldn't it? But instead it brings trouble and heartache, and all because two people are too proud to admit that they desperately need each other.'

'Love makes people vulnerable, *petite*. They erect barriers and once there are barriers there is warfare. It might be better if like the lower creatures we had hungers instead of ideals. Ah, there is Dick Travis who runs the stables!'

A stocky man with grizzled iron-coloured hair came out of a door, and as Gard began to question him, he thrust his hands into the pockets of his breeches and looked worried. Pierre hurried with Ynis to the two men. Gard swung to look at them. 'Dick says that Stella did go out on a chestnut, a horse called Rufus. Neither has yet returned, so it looks as if we must organize a search. Ynis, can you tell Dick exactly what you saw? Can you describe the place where it happened?'

She nodded and tried to keep her voice steady as she related once again all the painful details. Pierre must have realized that her legs were shaky, for he held his arm around her and acted more like her fiancé than Gard. She didn't blame Gard; she knew that his entire concern was centred upon Stella and the nightmare fate which could so easily be hers. It would be bad enough if the actress were only his friend, but she was loved by him with a complex passion that half frightened Ynis.

Love should hold a tenderness as great as passion, that burned itself into the bones and melted them.

As she looked at Gard's face and saw the lines etched deeply beside his lips and his eyes, she shrank closer to Pierre as if she belonged to him. She stood close in the circle of the Frenchman's arm and heard Gard say that he and Dick would organize the search for Stella. 'Take Ynis home,' he said to Pierre. 'Give her a stiff brandy when you get there.'

Pierre didn't argue with him about joining the search, and it was a relief for Ynis when they were in the car again and driving away from the stables. The sight and sound of the other horses made that scene on the moors too unbearably vivid. She sat deep in the seat which Gard had occupied and stared ahead at the road that took her back to Sea Witch. If she had not taken that walk to the stone on the moors she would now be on her way to London, unaware that Stella . . . oh, it was too awful to contemplate!

Last night in her sapphire blue she had looked so alive and mocking; the gay repartee so ready on her lips, and there in her eyes the bold intention never to let go of Gard to any other woman. It seemed to Ynis that in a shocking death Stella would hold him closer than any living woman could . . . he would remember her as Ynis was, laughing at his table all in blue, and raising a wine glass in mocking salutation to the engagement she had meant to break from the moment she had heard of it.

The car sped along the south drive and around by the terrace, where it stopped, and everything was quiet except for the cooing of the wood pigeons echoing across the lawns. Overhead, as they climbed from the car, the clouds were being combed into long wisps by the rising wind.

Pierre glanced at the sky and the grey light was caught in his grey eyes. 'It looks as if we might be in for a storm, which will make it all the harder for the searchers. Come, let us go inside and you must have that cognac which Gard prescribed for you. *Pauvre petite*, you look so tormented.'

'Who could have dreamed, Pierre, that such a thing could happen?' She walked ahead of him up the steps of the terrace, and her hair was tangled about her hollowed temples and cheekbones. She felt terribly awake and was acutely aware of everything, and yet it all seemed like a nightmare. 'What will we do if they can't find her and it has to be assumed that she has – oh, it will be ghastly for Gard. How will he endure it?'

'I can't say.' Pierre opened the glass doors of the morning-room and they went inside. 'It will be for you to try and console him—'

'How do I do that?' she cried. 'He has always loved Stella, and never for a moment has he loved me.'

'Do you love him?' Pierre asked quietly, and he didn't look at her as he went to the drinks cabinet and opened the flap. She stood half-way in the room, staring at him, hearing the clink of glasses just above the thudding of her heart. Denial rushed through her, but the words when they reached her lips had a curious defenceless sound.

'I'm grateful to Gard for giving me a home when I

needed one, but gratitude is no substitute for stronger feelings, is it?'

'What about compassion?' Pierre came towards her with the brandy glasses cupped in his hands. 'You are bound to feel that.'

'Thank you.' She accepted one of the glasses from him and studied the brown-gold liquid in the bowl. 'But it isn't passion, is it?'

'What would you know of passion, apart from what you have read in books? *À votre santé, petite.*' He touched his glass to hers and the crystal made a soft chiming sound. 'Drink up and blunt the edges of the nightmare.'

Her eyes dwelt wide and green on his lean worldly face. 'How do you know that I feel like that – awake in a nightmare?'

'From the look in your eyes, Ynis. You have speaking eyes and they reveal rather more than you would wish, perhaps.'

At once she shielded her eyes with her lashes, and lifted the brandy to her lips. It was cool against her lips, yet warm when it reached her throat, and the knot of tension slackened at her midriff as the brandy spread through her body.

'Does that feel better?' Pierre murmured, and she found that he had come a little nearer to her, and at once she retreated and sat down in the deep window seat. His charm was insinuating, and she felt sure his kindness was genuine, but all the same she gave him a cool little look which said: 'Keep your distance, you

131

dangerous Latin!'

He quirked an eyebrow and lounged on the arm of the leather sofa. 'If we sit and say nothing, then we shall only think of what may be happening out there on the moors. Shall we talk about passion, you and I? Sometimes to talk of it is more exciting than experimenting with it. Take this matter of bliss – to be fully appreciated it must also be painful. *Mais oui*, even though you wince at the idea. Those in love, and unsure, often assume a mask of coldness that can be a pain in itself. They mock each other, they speak words both careless and cruel. They would die of their secret pain rather than be unmasked.'

'It all sounds very tortuous,' she said, showing him her profile and assuming an air of indifference. 'Do you speak from experience, or from the angle of a playwright?'

'At my age, *jeune fille*, I have had my experiences. I have learned that love is the most subtle game in the world, and far more intriguing than a night at the gaming table, where one accepts defeat or victory with a gay laugh. No one laughs at love.'

'But surely you are talking about passion,' she rejoined. 'The hunt and the capture that always leaves you free to go stalking your next pretty bird.'

'Do you think I am stalking you, Ynis?' His accent gave her name a subtle attraction, making it seem foreign, and caressed. He made her very aware of his lean elegance, there at the corner of her eye, within reach of her hand. It would have been comforting to

132

press her face against a male shoulder, but she had already learned from Gard that she was neither child enough, nor woman enough, to enter a man's arms merely for comfort. It took more experience than she had to control the balance between kindness and kisses, and she still felt deeply shaken by the way Gard had reacted last night when she had resisted him. Even his lack of an arm had made little difference to his ability to control her struggles ... her first taste of the almost frightening degree of strength available to the aroused male.

At this moment she had no desire to find herself at the mercy of an ardent Frenchman!

'I am sure you are merely amused by me, *m'sieur*.' She said it demurely enough, yet her chin was tilted to let him know she meant it. 'With the more experienced girls of your acquaintance you can actually make a killing, but with me you have Gard to reckon with, and we both know that he has the power to alarm rather than the lesser ability to charm.'

'*Touché*.' Pierre inclined his head in quizzical acknowledgment of her ability to hold her own when it came to speech rather than actions. To look at she could be broken by a strong man; subdued by a determined one, but when given the chance to retaliate with words she wasn't at a loss. Pierre smiled at her, and the hunting light burned with a softer refulgence in his eyes, making of him an even more attractive man.

'There is honey and gall in most flowers,' he said, and his Latin accent made the words seem natural instead of flamboyant. 'Most men like a woman to be half angel, half rogue, and I believe most women like a man to be half devil and half saint. It balances, and being French I like things that are not extreme. Marriage itself should not be a compulsion; it should result from selection, and that is why I felt that Gard was doing the wise thing in choosing to marry a girl like himself, untouched emotionally, with passions unstirred.'

'You speak in the past tense,' she said, and she felt the locking of her fingers about the brandy glass. 'I – I don't want to believe that something awful has happened to Stella – but it must, and will, change things. It's only the living Stella whom Gard fights against, using me as weapon and shield. It's so strange. I just don't understand that sort of love.'

'Can you define the sort of love which would appeal to you?' he asked, leaning a little forward, intent and not in the least mocking.

'Not really,' she said. 'Whether it breathed fire and fury, or was merely tender, I should like it to be for my sake.'

'You want to be loved for yourself, eh?'

She nodded. 'It's asking a lot, I know—'

'Don't be so modest,' Pierre cut in. 'You are like your name, an island half wild and resistant to the hand of man. You are indeed young if you don't realize that not all men are inevitably drawn to the elegant product of a fashion salon.'

She gave him, then, a gravely amused smile. 'You

should see the wardrobe in my bedroom – at least imagine it, for I don't intend to take you there! It slides open from wall to wall, and is stuffed with fashionable clothes with tiny silk labels sewn into them, not to mention shoes, bags, and lingerie. Gard has tried his best – oh, I don't really know what he has tried to make of me!'

'Many another girl would say he was merely being very generous,' said Pierre quizzically. 'He has the money and little enough to do with it, here in the wilds of Cornwall.'

'You know the real truth,' she rejoined. 'Stella obviously adores clothes – and he chose to buy mine from the same fashion house as the one she favours. Last night he—' She broke off painfully, and was aware of Pierre staring at her.

'Go on, *petite*,' he murmured. 'Never leave a piquant sentence in mid-air like that, or you will give a Frenchman a jolt to his nerves.'

'This morning I was going to leave him.' She said it defiantly. 'I was half-way to the village when I – I saw the dolmen, there on the moors against the sky, like an enormous good luck stone, and I just wanted to touch it. It seemed to beckon, and when I reached it I heard the horse screaming—' She turned her sad-wild gaze to the windows and saw rain on the terrace. 'If only someone would come – or telephone! We talk, we try not to think, but we both know that screaming ourselves would help! It's a dreadful, cruel thing to happen to a poor animal – but Stella – she's so alive, so lovely – and

Gard loves her!'

As she said it, almost cried it, Pierre was on his feet and in a stride was there beside her. She felt the pressure of his hands on her shoulders and lifted her face to his; the silence between them seemed to hold a mutual cry from their hearts that Stella be safe from harm out there on the brooding moors.

'Pierre—'

'I know, *mon enfant*.' He sat down beside her and pulled her head to his shoulder. 'The waiting is always bad, all the more so for you because you saw the horse she must have been riding. So you meant to go away, eh? And where were you going?'

'To London – to any convent there that would take me in. My name is rather unusual, so there would have been some response to their inquiries before very long. It would be something, at least, to find out where I really belong. I sometimes think—'

When she paused, Pierre supplied the words. 'You believe that Gard knows more about you than he will tell, is that it?'

She nodded and felt the smoothness of his jacket beneath her cheek. He smelled clean and his skin emitted a slightly more aromatic after-shave than the one used by Gard. Everything about Pierre felt and was different from the feel of the man who had been so close to her last night, branding the shape and texture of his mouth on hers, and leaving the roughness of his hand on her skin. The hand that stroked her hair at this moment and found the slim nape of her neck was without that roughness, and that hint that it could be merciless.

'You are a nice child,' Pierre murmured. 'It might be easy for a man to want you; so tempting that he might lie to keep you. I have with you the feeling that one has in a quiet, secluded, very small chapel, where the stone sleepers lie so quietly on their shields, with lions curled at their feet. There is mystery in your face, Ynis. The dreaming quality of the Celt.' His fingers tightened, holding the nape of her neck as he pulled her head from his shoulder and brought her face just below his. He bent towards her, so that her hair ran between his fingers, and she was made defenceless by her need for tenderness. His lips travelled from her temple, down over the hollowed bone of her cheek to the corner of her mouth. It was curiously pleasant and not in the least alarming . . . she waited, almost like a sleeper, for his lips to touch hers.

But the moment lengthened and when she raised her eyelids he was gazing down at her with a rather pained expression on his lean, Gallic face. 'Not like that,' he groaned. 'With a sweet resignation, as if I am about to bless you. Are you like this with Gard?'

'How I am with Gard is none of your business!' She pulled fiercely out of Pierre's arms and gone like smoke was that sweet lethargy, that numb willingness to let him comfort her with a kiss. Men were all the same, they wanted it to be unwilling so they could hurt a girl! She jumped to her feet and as she did so the brandy glass rolled off the window seat to the floor. It looked drunken, and she felt her head spin as the strong cognac rose to her brain. She clutched at the curtain and was holding it like some tipsy creature when she saw figures appear on the terrace, solid and male, there in the fine grey mist of the rain.

One of them was leading the way, the other followed and in his arms he carried a woman . . . a woman whose loosened hair burned like a flame against the tweed of his jacket.

The french doors opened so suddenly, so forcibly, that Ynis was swept backwards as if on the tide of a powerful emotion. She was almost thrown against the wall, and there she stood, her green eyes fixed upon Gard as Dick Travis carried Stella into the room.

'Isn't it all very dramatic, my darlings?' Stella gave a throaty laugh. 'Like the start of the play . . . or the last scene before the curtain fall.'

CHAPTER EIGHT

IT was later that fraught day that Ynis learned from Gard more about the accident. She was sitting alone in the glass tower at the far end of the dimly lit hall when she caught the sound of his footfalls; she knew them for their deliberateness, their unswerving directness straight towards her. She tensed where she sat in a cane armchair, the pale colour of her dress lit momentarily by the strange flashes of lightning over the sea. She turned her head to watch the door open, and breathed the aroma of a cigar as Gard entered.

'I thought you had gone to bed until I caught a glimpse of you by the lightning through the glass,' he said. 'You seemed like a ghost, and like every old house in Cornwall this house has its ghost. I'm not unnerving you?'

'No,' she said, even as her hands gripped each other as he sat down on the windowsill near her chair and the smoke of his cigar drifted across her face. 'It's a strange storm. I keep listening for the thunder, but everything is so quiet.'

'It's sea lightning,' he murmured, and she could feel him looking down at her. With his back to the glass that was shaped into diamonds that rose all the way to the ceiling his face was in shadow and she couldn't see his expression, but her face and its look of tension was revealed by those flickers of steel-coloured light, an almost blue light that added mysteriously to the drama of the moment.

'How is Stella?' she asked quietly.

'Sleeping at last. She is one of those people who react to a pain-killing drug as if it were a glass too many of champagne. She just kept on talking, and I felt it better to let her react in that way, to get all the pain and alarm out of her system by letting her talk of the past until she felt exhausted enough to sleep. Tomorrow she will be able to act the lovely invalid to her heart's content.'

'The foot isn't broken?' As she spoke Ynis tried not to think again of that poor struggling horse, which had thrown Stella and left her on the moors with an injured foot.

'It's badly wrenched and she will have to rest for about a week. She must have been riding the horse pretty hard, of course, but Dick and I agreed not to chastise her. She knows what happened to the poor creature and has learned her lesson.'

'What, in not being cruel?' The words came uncontrollably from Ynis, and she wasn't a bit sorry for them.

'I know how you feel,' as he spoke he drew hard on his cigar and made the end burn angrily. 'You could never relieve your temper in that way. I believe you would sooner lay the whip across my back.'

'Perhaps.' Ynis shrugged. 'You and Stella understand each other, but I don't pretend to understand either of you. You and she deserve each other.'

'Do we really? And where do you come in?'

'I go, Gard, tomorrow.'

'Just like that, eh?'

'It would seem the best way. I've served my purpose of being whipping girl, and I've not liked it and don't want any more of the same. I must return to my own life, and you must tell me the way. I'm sure you know it.'

'Be sure of nothing, young woman, least of all that I intend to let you loose—'

'But, Gard, you must!' She jumped to her feet as the lightning licked across her tormented face. 'I shall only run away again—'

'Again?' He reached out and caught her by the wrist. 'What do you mean by that – were you running away when that bog tragedy held you back? Where the devil were you going? And what did you intend to use for money? I've made sure you have *things*, but I know you haven't any money.'

'*Things* can be pawned,' she reminded him, and all down the arm which he gripped with his steely fingers she could feel an unnerving tingle, as if the lightning had got into him and was being transmitted to her. 'And why should you care where I go? It isn't as if you—' The words stopped as if a hand of caution flung itself over her mouth, and the shock of what she had been about to say flared in her eyes.

'Let me go, Gard.' Her despair then was utterly quiet, for it was then, as his touch sent that curious thrill running through her, as they stood there in the glass tower like figures cut off from reality, that she fell in love with him. It struck her like lightning, so that she almost cried out, almost buckled at the knees from the shock of it. Even to breathe became a problem, for her heart was beating so furiously. Never had it been so essential that he release her from close proximity to him ... last night she had fought to get away from him, but now she was fighting her own impulses as she attempted to tear free of him.

'Oh ... don't!' Her shoulder almost felt wrenched as he jerked her so hard against him that she lost her balance and had to clutch at the empty side of him. Before when this had happened she had felt sheer disbelief that a limb could be so utterly lost. In this moment her entire body felt agonized with pity, so that she wished she could have stood in Stella's shoes and shown him that he wasn't physically repellent because he could no longer place two arms around a woman.

'You don't like to touch me, do you?' he mocked, and the lightning gleamed in his eyes as he looked down at her. 'I felt you shudder then as if you had put your hand into a flame. All right, there will be no marriage, so you don't need to run away. You can stay at Sea Witch and be unafraid that I shall force you into an unbearable situation. Poor young thing! All eyes and a heart that is beating fast enough to kill you.' Abruptly his arm encircled her shoulders and his chin rested against her slightly fevered temple. 'Yes, stay at

Sea Witch. There is nothing for you to go back to, and that is the truth.'

'But you know, Gard, where the place is.'

'Believe me, Ynis, you had left the convent when we met. You were living in rooms.'

'Alone?' she asked . . . this closeness to him could not conceal from her the tautening of his muscles, as if he braced himself to tell a lie.

'Of course, Ynis.'

'But I don't believe you!' She pulled away and he allowed her to do so. They stood looking at each other, and it was then that thunder rumbled over the rooftops and turrets of the house and echoed along its corridors. The glass panes rattled in the windows of the tower. A strange feeling passed over Ynis . . . something stirred awake in that part of her mind which had obstinately slept ever since that car had knocked her down.

'You must tell me the truth, Gard! What brought me to Sea Witch . . . and why do I almost seem to remember that you had some reason . . . not for loving me but for hating me?'

He stared at her without answering and the storm broke loose around them, pelting rain at the windows, and blazing through the panes the silver-blue lightning that almost burned the glass. It was as if all the distressing emotions of the day had built up to this; as if their human tensions were pitched against each other as the elements were pitched against the earth. This was their storm within a storm, her emotions striking against his, crying for the truth that lay on the lips she would never feel so demandingly ever again.

'I am sure that soon your amnesia will clear right away,' he said at last. 'I could rip aside the curtain right now, but I think your mind should do its own work. It will be better that way. Tomorrow the storm will be gone and the summer will begin. You must enjoy yourself. Be carefree. And I make only one stipulation.'

'I knew there would have to be one of those.' Braced to accept the truth, she felt an acute relief when he drew back on the very edge of revealing it. Tomorrow she might awake and remember everything, but tonight . . . tonight after all she wanted only the merciful blankness of mind.

'I should like you to continue in the role of my supposed fiancée,' he said, and he was very tall and upright against the streaming glass walls of the tower, sheathed in the black velvet of his smoking jacket. 'I promise that it will be only a pretence engagement from now on.'

'But I don't understand.' She gazed up at him with bewildered eyes. 'Surely you will want to tell Stella that what she saw in my room last night was a parody of the truth?'

'On the contrary, I want Stella to leave Sea Witch as soon as she is able.' He said it curtly, as if only in that way could he hide the truth of his feelings. 'She must return to her own life, and I must remain here to continue with mine. The past is done with, gone as my arm is gone.'

'But love remains.' The words broke from Ynis. 'You can't pretend that you feel nothing for Stella. She lingers and torments as some of the feeling persists where you once had nerves and muscles in your arm.'

'You seem,' he said quietly, 'determined to throw me into Stella's arms, as if only in that way will you be safe yourself from me. I do assure you that from now on it will be with us no more than a game of make-believe. I shall impose on you no more than the occasional smile of ownership, just to convince Stella that I intend to marry you.'

'Is your pride so unforgiving?' Ynis asked, and then she turned away so she couldn't see his dark face. Who was she to mention pride when she couldn't bear to mean so little to him? His fiancée of convenience and no more . . . she wanted to tell him to go to hell, to find some other scapegoat to bruise and use in his fight against his love of Stella. The woman he must send away because she couldn't live his life at Sea Witch, and he refused to return to the bright lights of theatrical London.

'It has nothing to do with pride,' he said. 'Nor anything more with my urge for a little revenge. You are too young, too lost, perhaps, for the real explanation.'

'No.' She shook her head. 'I know there is a love beyond love, and if you must use me—'

'I don't like you to use that expression,' he cut in. 'I am merely asking for your co-operation.'

'Why not? It's due to you in return for the care and the nursing I received when I was run down—'

'Ynis,' his hand touched her shoulder, and she could not control the quiver that ran all through her body, starting at the nape of her neck and winging its way to her very toes.

'Gard, may I go to bed?' Delicately she drew herself out of his reach. 'I'm feeling rather weary—'

'Weary of me and my demands, eh? Yes, shoot off, and don't worry any more. Tomorrow with any luck the sun will be shining and you can take yourself to the beach and paddle about in the rock pools.'

'Gard, I'm not a child!' She caught at the handle of the door and jerked it open. 'Perhaps I'll go to the beach with Pierre. He knows you were only being sardonic when you told him that your fiancée was sacrosanct.'

With these words she walked quickly away, leaving Gard in the cross-play of the lightning. When she reached her room it was as if all the fight ebbed out of her and she sank down on the tiger skin and buried her face against the snarling head of the beast. She lay there a long time and knew she was sublimating her desire for Gard by allowing her skin to cool itself against the thick, velvety fur.

The storm had died away by the time she went to bed, and she lay in the darkness listening to the raindrops falling from the creepers on to the stonework of the terrace.

Stay at Sea Witch, Gard had said. Don't be afraid

that I shall make any more demands upon you.

With a restless little groan she turned over in her bed and knew with every nerve in her body that she wanted him to make demands . . . loving demands.

Gard knew his Cornwall, and for the next week it was as if nature gave to Tristan's land a bonus of almost tropical weather.

Ynis felt as if she were living on the edge of a strange dream from which she could no longer escape by running away. The dream must hold her until the moment when Gard set free her body and held for always her wild young spirit.

She seemed as never before to belong to the wildness of Cornwall, and she was with Pierre a lot of the time, lending an avid ear to his worldly gossip, loving the high slithery silk of the Barbizon breakers. They didn't frighten her at all. She abandoned herself to the salt and shocking violence of the waves, half laughing and half screaming as they flung her sprawling upon the sands like a pale gold starfish.

She didn't know if Pierre had guessed that she and Gard were playing a game of make-believe. He never asked, but there were times when his eyes seemed to know the truth. She would catch a slight quirk to his eyebrow when in front of Stella the role of impatient bridegroom was played so suavely by Gard. He would touch her wrist, or look into her eyes, and even Ynis, who knew it was a game, had to fight with herself not to let her heart give away its secret.

She was aware that the sea air and the sunshine were lightly tanning her skin and making her green eyes glow. She knew this, and yet it made her feel so vulnerable when Gard paid her a compliment. It would be so wonderful if he meant it, but he said nice things only to fool Stella.

The residue of pain from her twisted foot had left interesting shadows under Stella's eyes, and her creamy pallor became her, softening the vitality of her face. Clad in rose-lilac, or cinnamon velvet, and at rest on one of the silk Empire sofas, she was a picture of desirability. She would pout at Gard and question him with her blue eyes, asking him silently how he could resist her.

Watching the play of eyes, feeling the cross-tensions, Ynis would be taut as a knife by the end of the evening. She slept badly and would be up with the dawn, racing through the dew-wet grass of the lawns to the steps winding down from the sea terrace to the shore. The mornings were so young and cool. Virgin, as she was virgin, running in the wind along the unmarked sands, feeling the silvery lash of the spray against her ankles.

The beach was flanked by great cliffs, and she would run and run until she came in sight of a lighthouse on a great serpent of rock curving out to sea. There were many rocks between the sands and the beacon, break-back, grey and tough, upon which the sea tore its silk. For hours she could have watched the waves, great plumes of light and energy, but inevitably she had to return for breakfast or invite Gard to come searching for her.

She had grown afraid of being alone with him, for the love she felt for him was growing stronger all the time, and being young, and so new to the emotion, she might give herself away. Her traitor body was finding it harder all the time not to respond to his touch, nerves leaping, like a young filly with only one master.

Her hair like a filly's tangled mane floated in the wind off the sea, and the incoming waves lapped about her legs as she walked back to the steps leading home to Sea Witch. Wild columbine and Cornish balm grew up the slope of the cliffs; foxgloves waved there, and golden gorse with tiny pea-heads. The air was balmy, blowing against her eyelids as she stood recovering her breath before going into the house. She met Alice in the hall and the maid at once informed her that Miss Marrick wished to have breakfast with her. 'She's in her room, miss. I've just taken a tray to her, with double helpings. She rang for me to do this. Mr. Gard has had to pop along to one of the farms and the French gentleman has taken him in his car.'

Ynis stood indecisive, pushing the hair back from her brow and looking, she knew, as if she had flown in on a broomstick. This summons to Stella's room, while Gard was absent from the house, could mean only one thing – the actress had decided to show her claws.

'Well, miss?' Alice was looking at her with a taunting little smile, running her eyes over her windblown hair, and the sandals she carried in her hand. 'Are you going directly to Miss Marrick, or shall I tell her you have to change and comb your hair?'

Temper stirred awake in Ynis, for ever since Stella's advent into the house the young maid had grown insolent, as if the staff expected any day to hear there had been a change in the master's wedding plans.

'I'm sure it won't turn Miss Marrick off her scrambled eggs to see me in a pair of jeans, Alice.' Ynis walked away barefooted from the gaping maid, and when she reached the door of Stella's suite she crossed her fingers and hoped she could hold her own now it had come to an open confrontation with the woman who was so much more adept at using the modern language of insult disguised as wit.

Still carrying her sandals in her hand, she knocked bravely on Stella's door.

'Do come in!' called the vibrant stage voice.

Ynis entered the room, with its white-panelled walls and deep peony-red carpet, and there in the grand bed with its canopy the figure of the actress, pillows banked behind her shoulders, and the peacock-blue of her robe brilliant against the white linen. If the robe was meant to remind Ynis of the night Stella had seen her with Gard, then the device was an effective one. She felt self-conscious as Stella swept a look over her, and arched a brow at her bare feet in the deep carpet.

'Have you been paddling?' she drawled.

'I enjoy walking on the beach in the early morning.' Ynis bent her head and fitted her sandals on to her feet, and she could feel the nervous beating of her heart. She should have gone to her own room instead of obeying the reckless impulse to show Stella that she wasn't afraid of her. She was frankly terrified and felt like making a bolt for her own room before this conversation went any further.

'The sands are so untouched and virginal, eh?' The insinuation in Stella's voice was not concealed. 'Do pull up a chair and have a cup of coffee. I do hope you like coffee in the morning? I always find tea a less stimulating beverage, but you probably prefer it.'

'Coffee will do,' said Ynis, and it took all her courage to carry a chair to the bedside and to sit so close to the silken rustle of the peacock sleeves and the whisper of Caron scent. To avoid a direct meeting with Stella's eyes Ynis studied the vanity table that was like an altar arranged for the worship of bodily beauty. The polished table below the wide mirror was laden with pots of all shapes and colours, and the glint of beauty implements in steel with ivory handles. Perfume preened in swan-necked flagons, and the sunlight reflected on the bold initials of the ivory-backed hairbrushes.

'Will you have some toast?' Stella took a slice from the silver rack and with superb composure she applied butter and a dob of honey, and all the time her blue eyes studied Ynis through the absurdly long eyelashes. She seemed amused by the younger girl's unpainted skin and casual hairstyle, and the brevity of her fingernails.

'I'm not very hungry.' Ynis sipped her coffee. 'Just rather dry.'

'I should have thought the sea air would make you ravenous.' Stella bit sensuously into her slice of toast. 'Are you worrying about something, my dear? It is an anxious time for a girl who is soon to be married. I understood that a designer and cutter was coming down from Town to fit your wedding gown – at least that was what Marc Honnet told me when I called in at the fashion house a few days before I came to Cornwall. What has happened, pet? Have you decided not to be married in white satin after all? Do you feel a little guilty, you with your convent upbringing?'

Ynis lowered her coffee cup very carefully into the saucer, and braved the taunting, curious, gem-hard quality of Stella's gaze. 'I am not Gard's mistress,' she said, with the simple frankness of the innocent. 'He would hardly need to marry someone he could have without the bells and confetti, and all that fuss.'

'Really?' Stella arched an elegant eyebrow and the movement of her breast stirred the Chinese birds woven into the silk of her robe. 'So you're holding out for marriage, are you? Well, you're cleverer than you look, or Gard is less impetuous. The man I remember was not to be held at arms' length by a mere woman—'

'I don't want to hear about it.' Ynis looked at Stella with youthful dignity. 'I know how Gard felt about you, but I know as well how much you hurt him at the time of his accident.'

'People can only be that hurt by those they love,' Stella rejoined. 'You don't run away with the idea that

Gard feels for you what he felt for me when I was your age. I could madden him, pet, until he had to shake me, or kiss me in the heather. It really was a pity that we were both so ambitious and talented. Our ambitions came like a sword between us for several years, but always that passion for each other was there, that driving need to fight and love. Can you bear to think of that on your wedding night, when he makes love to you and remembers instead the girl with titian hair whom he chased over the moors, his blood and nerves and desires linked in every way to hers?'

Stella paused to let these words sink into Ynis, into her mind and her heart. She lay back against her pillows, her titian hair loose against the Chinese silk of her robe, the heavy lids of her eyes betraying the desire she had for Gard, and the determination to win him back to her arms.

She had so much more beauty than Ynis, in a physical sense. She was like a species of exotic butterfly or orchid, and she made Ynis feel like a moth with unfledged wings. Looking at her, knowing that Gard had possessed her and could never forget her, made Ynis shrink into her shell, made secretly and terribly afraid that he would not resist her and let her go. Loving him now, so much, Ynis feared for him to be hurt again as Stella had hurt him before. He needed to be loved not as Stella remembered him, but as he now was.

'I think you only love yourself,' Ynis said bravely. 'Being loved by Gard, or any other man, is merely an extension of your self-love.'

'Mmmm, what a clever little miss you are!' Stella smiled, showing her white and perfect teeth. 'Being loved does stroke the ego, but there's a little more to it in this case, because we're talking about Gard, and he is something special. Married to the traditional girl-wife, he will stay here in the wilds and waste the artistic side of his nature. I mean to say, what do you know about great music and the thorough mastery of the whole craft which was Gard's? He's a Doctor of Music, an F.R.C.M. Is it all to be wasted on a little nobody? Would you see him waste himself ... when you love him?'

Pain seemed to shoot through Ynis when Stella spoke these words. With feminine intuition the actress had guessed the state of her feelings, so it would be futile to deny how she felt about Gard.

'He can never conduct again,' she said.

'No, but he can start to compose again.' Stella leaned a little forward and her blue eyes bored into Ynis. 'Why don't you go away and leave him to me? You know that it's really me whom he wants. He's fighting me for the sake of his pride. Trying to stem his love for me by using a bit of a thing like you to hold back the tide. Do you like that, being used by a man to keep another woman at bay? But then I expect you're flattered that he should even notice you, and we both know how you feel about him. And we both know that you could never keep him happy. He's too much for you, pet.'

'He's too good for you,' Ynis flashed. 'He has feelings, some regard for others, but you hadn't the heart enough to show him that he was still a great man at a moment when he needed that reassurance more than anything else in the world. I might not have your looks or your figure, Miss Marrick, but I know I have more heart.'

'All the more of it to break, you little fool, because I don't intend to give Gard up to you. *You*, the daughter of some petty little crook who tried to swindle Gard out of a thousand pounds! With your outlandish name it was easy enough getting on to who you really were, especially with my connections. Noel Raiford's daughter, and you talk to me about hurting Gard! On the day of his accident a little swine of a crook stole his wallet so they didn't know at the hospital that he was Gard St. Clair, the world-famous conductor. He should have been in clever, daring hands . . . oh, it was all such a criminal waste, and *you*, a criminal's brat, dare to sit there and call me heartless!'

Ynis sat there stunned, staring at Stella and trying not to believe that a word of it could be true. But there was something about Stella's face, a look of glittering triumph in the sapphire eyes, that told Ynis it was the dismal truth. While playing the helpless invalid the actress had been busy on the telephone, contacting people in London, press agents and journalists no doubt, who would have little difficulty in finding out the facts which amnesia had erased from the mind of Noel Raiford's daughter.

'Knowing how much Gard despises the petty criminal,' Stella went on, 'it strikes me as ironic that he should choose to become engaged to the daughter of one. But then there were always little things about him which I never quite understood – they only served to make him even more fascinating. I shouldn't want to know a man inside out, but I should like to know what you are going to do, Ynis, now the cat is out of the bag.'

'Where is – Noel?' Ynis could not yet remember the face of her father, but she felt the acceptance of his name on her lips.

'He was sent for trial and is serving his term at an open prison just outside Reading. He stole from Gard . . . are you going to follow in his footsteps and steal what doesn't belong to you?'

Ynis stared beyond Stella at the sunlight on the white panelled wall. The sun through the balustrade of the terrace cast shadows like bars . . . prison bars.

'Do you hear me?' Stella caught at her wrist and her long fingernails stabbed Ynis painfully. 'You know now that Gard couldn't possibly love you. Gard doesn't really want you, so what are you going to do?'

'I – I don't know.' Ynis wrenched her hand free of Stella's and felt the pain of being clawed. She jumped to her feet and backed away from the bed. Then she turned and ran from the room, slamming the door behind her and running . . . just running, out through a side exit into the fresh air, sky and lawns shimmering into a blur as tears rushed into her eyes. Blinded by tears, she ran full tilt into someone. Two arms gripped her, so the person wasn't Gard.

'*Chérie*, where are you going in such haste?'

'Pierre—' She raised a white, tear-streaked face to him. 'Gard never told me I had a father – I've just found out that my father's in prison!'

'And who has told you this?' Pierre ran his thumb across her wet cheek. 'It is probably a pack of lies.'

'No—' Ynis shook her head and her slim body trembled in his arms with the distress she felt, the shock, and the certainty.

'Was it Stella?' he demanded.

'Yes.'

'She is a bitch, that one. Come, child, to the car. We will drive until you are feeling better. Come!'

Encircled by his arm, she went with him to where his grey car stood in the drive. 'W-where is Gard?' she asked nervously.

'He has gone to the west wing to work in his study. There was a fire at one of the farms and now some forms to claim insurance must be filled in. There, climb in, make yourself comfortable and we will be off.'

'Pierre,' she spoke on impulse and her eyes were deeply pleading, 'will you take me to London? Will you take me away from here? I can't stay, not any more. I don't belong in Gard's house. My father stole from him, and now I know he hates me!'

'*Chérie*—'

'Please, Pierre!' She clutched at his arm. 'Suddenly I know where the convent is, it's at Bayswater, and I want to go back to it. I beg of you—'

'Don't beg,' he said huskily. 'Of course I will take you to London, but you must have a coat. It will start to get cold when the sun goes in, and the drive to Town is a long one. Wait for me. And dry your tears.' He tossed a large handkerchief into her lap, gave her a reassuring smile, and then made his way towards the house. As she wiped her eyes she heard the crying of the curlews drifting from the moors. The sound was like the crying of her heart.

CHAPTER NINE

THE day had gone and the evening lights were on in London when the silver-grey car sped through the Bayswater area, making for the Green which was on the opposite side of the road from the convent. It was strange how the memory of that old, lichen-walled house had returned to Ynis, exact as a painting, bringing with it remembrance of vesper bells, and the quiet Sisters in their grey robes. Of the hall where the pupils took their meals at the long scrubbed tables, and the enclosed garden where Sister Martha grew herbs and vegetables for the kitchen, and also rambling honeysuckle and tiny white roses.

It was unbelievable that she had ever forgotten the place where she had lived since a small child; in the heart of London, yet shut off from the bustle and the noise, and the drama.

'They wanted me to stay,' she told Pierre. 'Reverend Mother thought I should become a novice and eventually take the vows of Sisterhood. But somehow I couldn't—'

'Of course not.' He glanced at her as they waited below the glow of some traffic signals. 'You were not meant for the devotional life, not a girl with eyes like yours.'

Those eyes gazed up at him, heavy-lidded after the

long hours of driving, yet still holding a certain witchery as the green signal was reflected in them, so strangely shining, perhaps with the tears which had frozen within her as the miles stretched and Sea Witch was left far behind them.

The green light showed the pallor of her face and gave it a haunted quality.

'You are sure that you want me to take you back to these good nuns?' Pierre asked, as the car moved forward again. His A.A. map showed the location of the Convent of the Cross in Bayswater, and the sudden quick beating of Ynis's heart warned her that they were rapidly approaching the rambling old house shaded by the cypress trees planted long ago by the Franciscan monk who had blessed the convent when it was first opened. So old, so that she shivered a little as if a cold hand had touched her skin.

'I've nowhere else to go, Pierre. It's my only home.'

'Is it, *ma mie*?' He swung the car into a side road and there were the dark tall shapes of the trees shading the Green, where in the daytime mothers pushed prams, and dogs were let off the lead to scamper on the grass.

'I'm too tired right now to work out the meaning of that expression,' she said. 'I hope, Pierre—'

'I am the one to do a little hoping.' There was a quizzical smile in his voice. 'At the moment ours is a pleasant friendship which may grow deeper in a while – if you are not persuaded to take those vows.'

The light answer was on her lips when he suddenly

braked sharply and muttered a Gallic oath. Ynis sat up and stared from the car window. 'Oh no – it isn't possible! What has happened?'

Where the convent had stood there was now only the debris of a site being cleared for rebuilding. Red lamps glowed where the machines stood silent after their long day of pulling down the walls which had once enclosed the dormitories and the schoolrooms, the chapel and the kitchen. Gaunt heaps of brick lay where the vegetables and the flowers had grown. Only the cypress trees were left upright, as if someone had decided to let them live to screen the flats or offices that would be erected on the site.

A night watchman ambled over to the car and asked if they had lost their way. 'This was the Convent of the Cross?' said Pierre. 'We have not mistaken the place?'

'That's what it was right enough,' said the watchman. 'A new place in the country was provided for the nuns so this old place could be torn down. All the woodwork was rotting away, and the roof was in bad repair. It would have taken too much money to put the old place back in order, so they moved off, lock, stock and barrel.'

'To which part of the country did they go?' Still it was Pierre who asked the questions. Ynis was too stunned. It was as if all her hopes of finding a home were knocked down again with a cruel and desolate finality. The bells in the old chapel were stilled, the painted glass was broken, and the pall of dust had killed the little white roses. She was seeing her childhood in ruins, and she turned her face away.

'Ynis,' Pierre was touching her averted cheek, 'the old man says the Reverend Mother and her flock have moved to Northumberland. *Chérie*, I can't possibly drive you there tonight. You are worn out and hungry, and my road senses are dissolving.'

'I'm sorry, Pierre, for dragging you all this way on a fool's errand,' she said regretfully. 'I had no idea the convent was due to be demolished ... how sad it all looks, and the cypress trees add the correct funereal touch.'

'You must not be disheartened, Ynis. Tomorrow things will seem much brighter and your spirits will revive.'

'Funny,' she murmured. 'Gard said almost the same thing one night, when I talked with him in that glass tower at the end of the hall at Sea Witch. I – I asked him then to tell me the real truth about myself, but he said it would be better if I remembered the facts for myself. He had no right to keep it from me ... that my father was a crook.'

'Don't blame yourself for that.' Pierre spoke firmly and started the car. They drove away from the torn-down walls and the vanished security of the convent, and after a short while they were back on the main road, with its tall amber lights leading into the West End. 'You are your very own person, Ynis, and you will make your own life. You cannot carry the blame or the guilt for this crime of embezzlement committed by your parent. It has nothing to do with you.'

'It took me to Gard,' she said, a tiny note of bitterness in her voice. 'To beg him to spare Noel – but how could he do that? Noel was like the thief who stole his wallet – how could he forgive?'

'He couldn't,' Pierre agreed. 'It would not be human. It could not be asked of an angel, and Gard is neither saint nor devil.'

'I'm glad we were able to get away without seeing him.' Ynis sat low in her seat, wrapped in the rain cloak which Pierre had fetched her from the flower room. 'It would have made things difficult.'

'Difficult?' Pierre gave a soft, ironic laugh. 'My child, it would have made things dangerous. Better to scribble a hasty note, as I did, and make the retreat without rousing the enemy.'

'I – I don't want to think of him as an enemy,' she said. 'I know his motive in keeping me at Sea Witch was a strange one, but I'd sooner believe he felt sorry for me than that he meant me any harm.'

'*Il n'est pas méchant*,' murmured Pierre, as the car swept into the bright and fantastic lights of the West End, where seductive murmurs and aromas seem to perpetually steal from the dim doorways of the French and Italian restaurants. 'Life played a hell of a trick on him, snatched from his very hand the magic wand of success, and now it is for him *une vie dure*. Not in the sense that he faces hardship, but life is making him hard.'

Ynis sat folded into her cloak like a nymph-moth

163

which had returned to the chrysalis. She felt unbearably sad, and her face reflected this as the gay lights flickered in and out of the car as they sped along Shaftesbury Avenue.

'Shall we go and eat at a small restaurant?' Pierre asked.

'I – I don't really want to.' The thought of sitting in a public place, with curious eyes upon them, made her shrink into an even smaller heap. 'I'm wearing jeans, Pierre. I feel too untidy.'

'Then we had better go straight to my apartment,' he said.

She cast a look at him. 'Your apartment?' A note of alarm jarred in her voice, a tiny whisper of doubt stirred through her mind. Now it struck home forcibly that she was all alone in London with him, with no money in her pocket, and nowhere to sleep ... unless she allowed him to decide the matter for her.

'I can't take you to a strange hotel and leave you there,' he said, in a calm, deliberate voice. 'You have no clothes, no suitcase, and hotels make a quaint rule about these things. My apartment is the best solution. It is comfortable, warm, and there are two bedrooms. I do assure you, *petite*, that after driving all these hours I am not feeling at my most amorous. Now what do you say?'

'What can I say, except thank you for all your kindness.' She gave a rueful little laugh. 'Being brought up in a convent is not the very best way to learn about men. We should think of them as angels, but instead we tend to think of them as satyrs.'

'Let us blame it on your unfortunate encounters so soon after coming out into the wide and wicked world.'

'My father – and Gard,' she said quietly. As she thought of Gard her heart seemed to contract like a flower struck by frost. She had thought that disillusion could strike out love as if it had never existed, but the love was still in her being and her very bones, a pain and a strange unwanted pleasure as the image of his dark face grew in her mind until the haughty features and the mocking mouth seemed poised above her, bending slowly to her lips.

'We are almost home.' Pierre must have felt the way she shivered. 'Soon you will be drinking hot coffee and sitting in front of a fire.' He turned the car into a quiet square in Albany, with tall lamps at either side of the road, reflecting on to the elegant doorways and the tall Georgian windows of the apartments. He parked the car and assisted her from her seat, gripping her hand reassuringly as they made their way along a paved path bordered by flowers and with a curving roof above it, with scrolled iron lamps attached. It was all so quiet that their footsteps sounded overloud on the stone stairs leading to his front door. They passed some plaques attached to the pale walls, and there was a white stucco bust of Byron quite near to the doorway of Pierre's set of rooms.

He unlocked the door and switched on the hall light. There were long curtains beside the Regency windows, and several lovely old prints of Georgian London on the walls. They entered the living-room and once again the spring of light revealed curving windows, warm, rich colours, elegantly striped wallpaper, and a serpentined sideboard of dark oak.

Ynis, still a little dazed by their long drive, stood absorbing the serene atmosphere of the apartment. It was unexpected, less modern than she had expected, and it revealed a firm liking for the finer things of life.

'Let me take your cloak.' He removed it from her shoulders with all the charm and courtesy of a Regency buck, and she looked at him quickly with her green eyes, and a smile trembled on her mouth.

'I spoil the illusion with my jeans. I'm sorry, Pierre.'

'You spoil not a thing, *chérie*.' He said it lightly, but when he looked into her eyes an awareness of their aloneness was taut as a fine wire between them.

'I'm sure I look a sight!' She turned away and saw herself at once reflected in a circular mirror set deep in a honeycombed frame. It was the kind of mirror which should have reflected elegance, but her hair was tangled about her white face, and her eyes looked huge and hunted, like those of a fugitive! 'Oh dear, I look worse than I thought!'

'. . . *nursed in whirling storms. And cradled in the winds,*' he quoted above her head. 'Yes, I think you are *the offspring of a dark and sullen sire.*'

She lifted her hands and pushed the brown hair back

166

off her brow. 'I suppose you think I'm crazy, running off without a penny piece, or a change of clothing?'

'Neither need be a problem, Ynis. If you will put yourself in my hands.'

'Meaning?' She studied his face reflected in the mirror behind her own face. She wasn't a child and had grown up almost too quickly in the past twenty-four hours. There was something ruthless about the emotions between men and women . . . men were not kind merely for the sake of it.

'*Faîtes comme vous voulez.*' He half smiled. 'My home is at your disposal and you may do whatever you like in it without feeling under obligation to me. Now what is your first wish, *madame*?'

'A bath.' The words sprang to her lips eagerly. 'I should love one of those more than anything else! I feel as crumpled as a piece of old wrapping paper.'

'That is a very easy wish to grant. Come!' He took her hand and led her out of the door, across the hall and into the bathroom. He switched some switches, turned on the hot water tap, and then gave her a slight bow. '*Voilà.* Within a matter of minutes everything will be warm and the water will be hot. There in that corner cupboard there are bath towels, there on that shelf are soaps and crystals, and the matter of a comfortable change of clothing can also be arranged if you don't mind wearing a pair of pyjamas which a travelling aunt sent to me and which turned out to be a size or two too small?'

'Pierre, you *are* kind.'

'Don't say it so emphatically, as if you need to convince yourself.' His own smile held a touch of irony as he flicked his fingers against her cheek. 'I will let you into a little secret about yourself, Ynis. Your chaperone, *ma petite*, is your beguiling innocence, apart from which you have the priceless gift of being pleased by a little kindness, and it would be like taking candy from a child to rob you of that pleasure, and to rob myself of the good feeling it gives me to be nice to you. I will now go and cook a large and tasty omelette, my one and only accomplishment in the kitchen, while you soak the weariness from your bones.'

He departed and she took a pleased look around the bathroom. She liked the lemon-coloured tub and the gay tiling. The lambswool rug and the array of gaily coloured bottles on a glass shelf. How different it all was from the austerity of the bathrooms at the convent; there had been no rails to warm the towels, no pine-scented crystals to fill the air with such a refreshing aroma.

She gave a little start as fingers drummed the door. She opened it and there was her host again, offering her the pyjamas and a dark silk robe. 'You can roll up the sleeves,' he said. 'Take your time – sing if you wish.'

'*Merci*, Pierre.' She smiled and took the change of clothing. 'I'm afraid I haven't a very musical voice.'

'I shan't hold that against you.' He lowered the lid of his right eye in a wink, and then withdrew. She examined the pyjamas and found them to be of a gaily hued silk with a dragon on the breast. She was glad they were gay. The gaiety took away the sense of intimacy in wearing a bedroom garment belonging to a man.

She removed her jeans and shirt, and her underskin tingled and it felt good to relax and to feel in a while the tiredness seeping out of her limbs. The foamy pine bath eased away the aches of her body, even if the heartache remained. She couldn't ignore that subtle pain which had nothing to do with her physical self. It was there inside her, the shock of learning that Gard had reaped some strange, perverse satisfaction out of keeping her at Sea Witch, the daughter of a man he had sent to prison. She lay there in the comfort of the water, body eased and yet bewildered. Each time he looked at her he must have hated her because her name was Raiford ... he had not known that Noel had been her mother's husband, but he had not been her father. She had learned this salient fact at the convent when she was fifteen. Reverend Mother had thought she should be told on account of Noel's criminal tendencies.

'I don't want you to grow up, child, believing you might have the same immoral character.' How well Ynis now remembered those words! 'To take from others is a sign of weakness. To give is strong and blessed.'

The little sermon had been of comfort. It had also planted in her heart the hope of helping Noel to be a better person. She remembered how she had pleaded with Gard to drop his charge against Noel ... she hadn't known that he had every reason to despise the petty cheat; every right to expect that person to pay for his crime.

She released the water from the tub and used the hand shower to rinse the soap off her skin. Then she stepped over the side to the lambswool rug and wrapped a warm towel around her body, the ends of her hair clinging wet to her neck. She stared into the mirror that stretched along the wall, half shocked by the reflection of herself. She had never been a girl to dream of men and love, like others at the convent. She had never thought of herself as someone to be noticed, and curiosity stirred within her when she thought of Pierre, who had taken the trouble to bring her all this way to London, driving all those miles, and stopping only a short while so they could eat a quick meal.

Was Pierre intrigued not by her looks but by her so apparent innocence? Did he find it novel to have on his hands a girl whose knowledge of men was divided between a jailbird whom she barely knew, and an embittered man of music, whose desire for love was without tenderness?

She patted talc all over her and found that it had a pleasant aroma despite its masculine label. Pierre was a man of discriminating taste, who had obviously planned his life to be in tune with his worldly temperament. As the silk tunic of his pyjamas slid down over her pale skin and settled on her slim thighs she turned away from the look of seduction which the mirror gave back to her. If Pierre were to see her like this . . . oh, but he mustn't!

She stepped quickly into the silk trousers and tied the cord very firmly. She put on the robe, rolled up the long sleeves, and felt more satisfied with the absurd picture she now presented. It was safer to look foolish rather than fetching, and she gave a tiny grin as she picked up the comb and ran it through her damp hair. It clung straight and dark about her head ... little clown, she thought, and wondered if Gard had been very angry when he had found Pierre's note of their hasty departure. Just a few lines, Pierre had told her, to let Gard know that she was returning to the convent.

Suddenly a slight frown knitted her brows. She wondered if Gard had known that the Convent of the Cross was to be erased ... he had denied knowing exactly where she came from, but there was a remote possibility that he had wished to spare her the knowledge that her home for so many years was to be destroyed.

Then she shook her head ... no, he had just wished to keep her in the dark about herself so that her feeling of dependence upon him would be all the more acute. He had given her things, and he had even made love to her ... had he hoped she would love him so he could hurt her as Stella had hurt him?

Had that motive been at the root of the situation all along? Would he even have gone as far as marriage with her in order to give full rein to his bitterness ... the accumulated pain and passion of a man who had seen his whole life's work snatched from him just as triumph and the woman he loved were in his grasp? It seemed terrible to Ynis that a man could be so bitter, and yet she couldn't hate him for it. After all, to him she had been only the daughter of Noel Raiford, there to be hurt so his own deep pain could be eased.

Suddenly her thoughts were unbearable and after making the bathroom as tidy as she had found it, she let herself out and went across to the door of the living-room. When she opened the door she couldn't suppress a little murmur of delight. The fire had been lit and a small table for two was set in front of it, with wine glasses beside the plates and cutlery, and the soft light of a standard lamp falling across the table. Pierre was not in the room so she guessed he was still in the kitchen preparing their supper. By comparison to Gard he was so uncomplicated, so charming without being sardonic about everything. Feeling rather like a pampered child, for probably the first time in her life, Ynis made her way to the fireside where a hassock was hunched as if waiting for her. She sat down on it and held her hands to the warmth of the coal fire, and looked about her rather like a child who couldn't believe in the reality of her surroundings.

Everything was so quietly elegant and harmonious – the gold striping of the walls, the long low sofa covered with brocade, the flanking turquoise chairs, the supper table, and the sliding Spanish grilled panels that concealed the cocktail bar.

Just a few feet away from her on a bookshelf stood a china bird in a tree of china flowers and leaves. The books had lovely old bindings, and on the wall above were miniatures of Regency ladies with demure faces and intricate hairstyles.

She was smiling at the charm of the room when Pierre entered carrying a tray of Georgian silver on which stood a lovely old coffee jug and the omelette under cover. Ynis turned her gaze from the fire to look at him and the smile still clung to her lips, while in the warmth the ends of her hair were beginning to curl against the pale skin of her neck.

'Good! You are looking much more relaxed.' Pierre had changed into a casual cardigan and slacks, and there was a lazy look of pleasure in his grey eyes. He placed the food on the table, and the aroma of the French coffee stole to Ynis and made her suddenly realize how hungry she felt. She had hardly eaten anything when they had stopped on the road, but now she stood up eagerly and came to the table.

Pierre sliced the omelette in half and as he served her, mushrooms and other delicious-looking mouthfuls tumbled out of the golden envelope. 'I am proficient, no, with a can-opener and an egg-beater? Alas, we have no bread, but I found a packet of cheese straws.'

'It looks superb, Pierre.' She tucked in hungrily and heard him give a satisfied laugh. He poured the coffee and sat down facing her, and as he took the edge off his own appetite she could feel his eyes upon her, amused, and perhaps a little speculative.

'I hope you feel quite comfortable in the pyjamas?' he said. 'I am glad now that I didn't send them to a bazaar. Perhaps I always hoped that some night a charming young woman would wear them to eat supper with a lonely bachelor.'

'I'm not naïve enough to believe that you often eat supper alone,' she scoffed.

'You mean to say you believe what Stella said about me?' He looked mock-injured. 'You must know by now that Stella is not exactly kind about her friends. Her enemies are frankly terrified of her.'

'Yet Gard loves her, even yet,' Ynis murmured. 'It must be quite something to be loved for your sins, your sorrows, and not alone for your virtues.'

'It must indeed.' Pierre pushed aside his empty plate and leaned his elbows on the table, his chin on his folded fists, his eyes directly upon Ynis, who was still nibbling cheese straws. 'Is that the kind of love you are hopeful of finding, Ynis?'

'I – I don't think about love,' she said airily. 'I'm quite young and I have to think about other things. A job, for instance.'

'Ah,' his eyes glinted, 'are you not going to the nuns in Northumberland?'

'No, I think I want to stay here in London. It's time I cut the habit strings, isn't it? I can't keep running back to Reverend Mother each time a crisis comes along in my life. I might as well take vows if I'm going to panic each time I meet a man like—' She broke off and poured herself some more coffee. 'I wonder what I do about finding a job? Apply to the labour exchange, I suppose?'

He nodded, but the narrowing of his eyelids told her that he knew her panic was caused by Gard and not by himself. Fear was first cousin to love, and she prayed that he wouldn't guess that she had committed the folly of falling in love with the dark St. Clair.

'Did they teach you any of the vocations at the convent?' he asked. 'If you can type and take dictation then you could work for me. I don't demand shorthand, only a legible hand that will enable my dialogue to be transcribed with exactitude.'

'Haven't you a secretary already, Pierre?' She liked the idea of working for him, but it all sounded too good to be true. There had to be some obstacle to such a perfect solution to her problem.

'I had a secretary,' he corrected her. 'She was a young woman whose services I shared with Stella. Contrary to what Stella told you about Lucy, it was not I who caused her to run out on the job in tears.'

Ynis held her coffee cup in her hands and gazed over the rim at Pierre with large grave eyes. 'One day,' she said, 'someone will treat Stella like Desdemona and strangle her.'

'Are you nominating St. Clair for the role of Othello?' Pierre asked quizzically.

'It could happen, couldn't it?' Her heart felt terribly heavy in that moment, as if with foreboding. Her green eyes clouded over. 'They do seem like lovers who can't be happy together or apart. Oh, why couldn't she leave him alone? Let him find some kind of peace with his Sea Witch. Better to love a ghost than to be continually haunted by the living woman who won't let him forget yesterday; who keeps reminding him of his success and the glamour of being her fiancé.'

'How was it for you, Ynis, when he was *your* husband-to-be?' Pierre spoke casually enough, but she sensed the depth of curiosity behind the question. The desire to be assured, perhaps, that her heart was as untouched as her body.

'It was all a masquerade, you know that. He even gave me Stella's ring to wear – the ring he chose for her that day in Oxford Street. He loved her so much that he couldn't forgive her for being repelled by his mutilation. It was as if she unmanned him. But no woman could do that to the Gard he has become since the accident. He's like one of those stone dolmens on the moors, gigantic when he stands over a woman, and terribly hard. If I loved a man,' her gaze left Pierre and dwelt on the china bird in the china tree, 'I couldn't be repelled by anything that happened to his body, but I could be turned away by a heart of stone. If Gard marries Stella, she will be getting a man she deserves, for Gard's heart has turned to stone.'

'Tell me,' Pierre rose to his feet, 'have you ever heard his music?'

She shook her head. 'I knew he had a collection of his recordings at Sea Witch, but he always kept them locked away.'

'We will drink our wine beside the fire, eat the white peaches which I have cooling in the fridge, and listen together to a recording which may help you to forgive him, a little.'

'I'd like that,' she said, and kept to herself the fact that she had already forgiven Gard. Now when she went to the hassock beside the fire some of the former charm of the room had seeped away and a sudden melancholy clung round her like a garment. She stared into the fire, blinking her eyes catlike at the small spurts of flame. If you drew too close to love, if you touched the beauty of the flame, it only burned you in return and left you wary of reaching out again.

She shrank into herself as Pierre came to her side and placed a glass of wine in her hand.

'A pale Ste. Croix du Mont, just the wine to go with the peaches which I found in the cupboard. Lucy sometimes did my shopping for me and she was rather fond of tucking these canned exotics among the sardines and the lump sugar.'

'Lucy sounds as if she were fond of you.' Ynis looked into her wine and not at him. 'But it isn't wise to get too friendly with a secretary, is it? You and I must be more formal when I start to work for you.'

'So you want to work for me?' He bent and put a finger under her chin and made her look at him. 'You really would like that, eh?'

'Yes, so long as it's strictly on a business basis.'

'You funny child,' he sighed. 'You sit there in my robe and pyjamas, a glass of French wine in your hand, and you expect me to be distant with you.'

'It will be easier when I am behind a desk, taking dictation.'

'But you are so oddly charming, Ynis. Almost a small sketch by Rembrandt with your brown uneven hair and your eyes that are green and pointed as young leaves.'

'You should put those lines in a play, Pierre.' She gave a laugh and drew herself out of the reach of his hand. 'Let me drink my wine.'

'You must have a peach with it.' He turned to the table and with a small silver knife he sliced the peaches into halves. He placed the plate within reach of her hand, then went to the radiogram, a very modern piece of equipment concealed within a lovely old cabinet. Ynis watched him, and felt the quick, almost violent beating of her heart as he took a record from an album. He gazed at the label for a long moment, then he placed the record on the turntable of the radiogram.

'This is a recording made by Gard of Isolde's *Liebestod*, which he arranged himself for the organ. There, are you ready to listen?'

She nodded, for she couldn't have spoken a word. It was as if Gard were about to enter the room.

'I will turn out the lamps and we will listen to the music by the firelight.'

The room went dim and in that moment the music began. Ynis closed her eyes, as if to visualize him alone in a great, arched chapel, seated at the great organ below the religious windows, looking like Milton's devil-angel as he played the dying love song of Isolde, the faithless wife of a Cornish king.

How appropriate the music, how dramatically alive

with the beauty and the doom of the Cornish landscape!

How beautifully he played, as if then he had more heart than other men. The effect the music had upon her was akin to physical pain . . . this was Gard making music with hands so supple and vibrant on the keys of the organ, so sure and strong . . . so doomed this music to be made only for a while, at the height of his talent and his fame.

As the final soaring notes died away, a silence of sadness and tribute settled over the Regency room, and the man and the girl seated beside the fire that threw its soundless shadows on their faces. The clock ticked on the mantelshelf, and somewhere in the night a motor bike passed with a muted roar along the Marlborough Road.

The reality of the sound broke their silence and as he pressed the switch of a small lamp on the sofa beside him, she felt his eyes searching hers, looking perhaps for a sign of tears. Instead there was a blaze of fury in her eyes.

'It was so unfair,' she cried. 'Of all the people in Oxford Street that morning, why did fate have to pick on him?'

'So that he might pay his dues to the jealous gods, *petite*. The Greeks always claim that the gods grow angry when a mortal has a touch of genius. Gard had it, there is no doubt of that, and so they smote off his arm and made him like other men.'

'He will never be quite like other men.' She rose to

her feet, and now her face showed her tiredness. 'I should like to go to bed, Pierre. It has been a long day – a strange day.'

'First won't you finish your wine?' he coaxed. 'If you go to bed too tired and fraught, then you won't sleep. You will toss and turn till dawn. The wine will blur your senses – try it.'

'All right.' She raised the glass to her lips and drank the wine quickly. She wanted above all to sleep and forget, and to wake in the morning, perhaps, with the ache at heart less acute than it was right now.

'Please, I'd like a drop more,' she said, and held out her glass. He poured it for her and watched her as she drank it. 'It's very good, Pierre—' And then her head began to whirl and her legs felt funny. 'Ooh, I do feel odd – d'you suppose I'm tipsy?'

'After swallowing a couple of glasses of wine in that quick fashion I would say yes.' His arms collected her and he lifted her off her feet. He carried her from the living-room and across the hall, and she felt so blessedly numb and inert that she didn't protest as he carried her into a small bedroom and lowered her to the bed. He drew off her shoes and removed the robe, and she blinked her eyes at him and was already half asleep.

'You're so kind, Pierre.'

'So you keep telling me.' He drew back the bed-covers and rolled her into the bed.

'Your hair looks so nice, Pierre. Like a halo.'

'And how about my wings?' he murmured, tucking her in. 'Do you like those?'

'Yes, they're very becoming.' She snuggled her cheek against the pillow and it felt so good to be tucked in like a child. 'Sister Yvonne used to do this sometimes, just as a treat, but we weren't really allowed to be spoiled.'

'Ah, *mon enfant*, you have not been spoiled nearly as much as you deserve.' He bent over her and she felt the warm brush of his lips across her cheek. 'Good night, young maiden. Sleep serene in your virtuous bed.'

'Good-night, Pierre. See you in the morning.'

'Yes, in the morning we must see about getting you some clothes, and finding you somewhere to live. *Bonsoir, chérie.*'

'*Bonsoir, m'sieur chevalier.*'

The light went out and the door closed behind him, and it was then that the tears crept down her cheeks. The music had been so lovely, but it had been like the dying song of her own love for Gard. It had to die if she was to make a new life for herself in London ... with Pierre.

When she awoke in the morning it was broad daylight, and there was a note propped against the little clock on the bedside table. She sat up rubbing her eyes and tumbling her hair with her hands. Half past nine! Heavens, she had not slept so late since those slow, long days of her recovery from being knocked down. She reached for the folded note and propped on her elbow she read it. '*Chérie*, I have gone to see my agent, and on the way home I shall see if there are any flats to let, and buy a *poulet* for our lunch, and a dress for you to wear. I hope you can cook!'

She smiled, and then she sighed a little and pushed aside the bed-covers. She went to the bathroom, where she found her jeans folded over the hot rail, and her shirt and underthings arranged on the stool. Pierre was the most thoughtful person she had ever met, and yet again she sighed.

She made coffee and toast in the kitchen, and sat there staring out of the window at the courtyard gardens. They were very quiet and neat, and she supposed that children and their dogs would not be allowed into premises like these. She washed her cup and saucer, and then she wandered across the hall to the living-room. By daylight it looked more formal and she much preferred it when the lamps were alight and the coal fire was glowing. They warmed the pale gold walls and the curtains.

She was by the bookcase, admiring the china bird in its china tree, when the telephone suddenly rang and she almost jumped out of her skin. She went out to the hall and lifted the receiver. 'Hullo,' she said, and gave the number on the dial.

For about half a minute there was dead silence at the other end of the line. Then: 'Is that you, Ynis?' Her name thundered against her ear-drum, and every nerve in her body responded to that well-known voice. She went as still as a creature in a thicket, pursued but still wildly hopeful of eluding the hunter.

'Yes,' she said defiantly. 'I'm here with Pierre, and I'm perfectly happy, so you needn't concern yourself about me any more.'

'Don't be a child,' he rapped.

'Don't call me a child,' she retorted. 'You heard me say that I'm here with Pierre, at this apartment. I'm going to work for him, so you needn't worry that I'll go on the wrong road like Noel. Please give my regards to Stella, and thank her for putting me wise.'

'Ynis, don't hang up! Half the night—'

'I am pretty sure that you were wild with me for leaving Sea Witch before you could have the pleasure of seeing my face when I remembered that first night – all the grovelling I did for Noel's sake.' She took a deep breath. 'Well, it's all over now, Gard. I'm with Pierre and he's kind to me.'

She hung up quickly, and then backed away from the telephone as if it could strike at her, curled like a black snake there on the hall table. She turned away and there in a wall mirror was her white face staring at her, and her green eyes blazing with shock and temper, and a wild, wild sadness. Why did he have to matter so much? Why couldn't she feel this stormy longing for Pierre, who was kind, and not made bitter by the awful, unforgivable things which had cast such a shadow over Gard's life? With Pierre there could be gaiety, and petting, and wine with peaches. But as a cold little shiver snaked all through her body, she knew that what she wanted, with every fibre of her being, was the tang of gorse, the chill of the sea on a dark cheek, and eyes so dark they drowned her.

She fled to the living-room and huddled on the sofa as if for warmth. There was coal in the scuttle, and wood shavings, and she could have lit the fire, but she felt an utter disinclination to ever move again. If only like a moth she could tuck in her wings and shrivel into dust!

How long she sat like that she never knew, but what aroused her from her apathy was the sonorous demand of the front door chimes. She sat up, smoothed her hair, and then made her way to the door. Pierre was probably laden with parcels and couldn't manage to open the door with his key. A second before she opened the door to let him in, she forced a smile to her lips.

She flung open the door . . . and the smile froze on her mouth, and the French name gave way to another that was so different. '*Gard!*'

'Yes,' he growled. 'In person.'

He strode past her into the hall of the apartment, big and dark in a trench overcoat that swung from his broad shoulders like a cloak.

'What are you doing here?' she demanded. 'I – I thought you were phoning long-distance.'

'I was calling you from Paddington. I have just come from there in a cab.' He stared down at her as she stood there by the open door, raking her shocked white face with his dark eyes. They held an almost frightening blaze, those unforgettable eyes of his. They were the only things alive in his stony face. 'Shut the door, Ynis. There is a draught from those stone stairs.'

'What do you want, Gard?' She let the door slam shut, but she made no move away from it, as if it represented a means of escape from him. 'I told you over the telephone that I am going to work for Pierre. It's what I want—'

'Is it really?' And then the most unbelievable thing happened ... that bold and rather beautiful mouth that so rarely smiled was smiling now, gently, without the mockery, or the sardonic twist to the lips. 'Half the night I've been travelling from Cornwall, but believe me, Ynis, I didn't come all this way to hear you say that you want to be a typist. May we go into the lounge? Standing here in the hall makes me feel as if I've come to check the gas meter.'

For one tightrope instant Ynis almost told him to go to hell with his wisecracks, and then uncontrollably she was smiling herself. 'You are the unsaintly limit, Gard! You're always giving orders, cracking the whip, telling me what to do.'

'Is this the lounge?' He pushed open a door, and there was the room in which she had slept, the single bed still thrown open, and the dragon pyjamas bright against the covers.

'You've been here before,' she said witheringly. 'You are just checking to see if I slept with Pierre. Oh, God, I'd like to do something to really shake you—'

'Come in here.' His hand had hold of hers before she could retreat out of his reach and he pulled her into the Regency room. The trench coat dropped from his shoulders to the carpet, and she half-closed her eyes in

185

pain and love and acutest longing as she saw again that firmly pinned sleeve.

'Do you think it didn't shake me when I found that note of Dumont's and realized you were gone, Ynis?' His eyes blazed down into hers, holding her as still as a bird. 'For hours on end I tramped the moors, telling myself it was better that you were out of my way. Free of a man who hurt you when he felt like it and used you for his own embittered purpose. Yes, I wanted to show Stella that she could no longer hurt me, so I used you, flaunted you in front of her, dressed by her own coun- turier. With the arrogant assumption that I had the right to your person, because your father had robbed me—'

'He isn't my father!' She just had to let him know that she wasn't the child of the man he justifiably de- spised. 'He married my mother when I was little more than a baby. When she left him, and left me on his hands, he placed me at the convent. Now the convent is gone, a heap of rubble in Bayswater – that was why Pierre brought me here to his apartment. He's been so kind—'

'As damnably kind as I have been unkind, eh?'

She nodded, for it was only the truth. 'You really could have saved yourself a long journey, Gard. My memory is back, and I'm not going to go on blaming you for thinking I was a chip off Noel Raiford, to be despised and used by you. Let us forget it. You have Stella – and I have my job with Pierre to look forward to – *Gard*!' His name was a little scream as his finger.

convulsively gripped her wrist and almost broke her bones. She went terribly white and the room swayed around her . . .

'Ynis – child.' Her hand was at his mouth, pressed there like an injured bird, and his eyes were alive with the horror of hurting her. She had never seen such a look on his face before . . . he had gone deathly white under the swarthy suntan, even to his lips. The lines in his face were as detailed as if slashed there by an etching knife. 'Girl, why do I go on tormenting you when all I want – all I want—'

'Tell me, Gard.' She still felt uncertain, but a wild, wild hope was knocking at her heart, and the pressure of his lips was drawing the pain from her hand. 'Oh, tell me!'

'All I want is to love you.' He said it against the throb of her pulse, as if his lips would burn their way through her skin, to her heart itself. 'It's too late, of course. I should have told you at Sea Witch, while I still had the hope of holding you. Now you want that good-looking Frenchman, with his charming accent, his courtly manners – and his perfect body!'

'Don't, my darling!' With all the hunger of her own body she wrapped her arms about Gard, pressing close to the mutilated side of him, as if to enter his heart if she could. 'Dearest devil—'

'Don't pity me,' he said curtly. 'To hell with that from a woman!'

'Pity you?' she scoffed. 'It would be like trying to bottle a storm to soothe you down with kind words and custard. You aren't half so nice as Pierre, and your manners are abominable at times. I'm still trying to figure out why I fancy you—'

'You what?' His voice was a dangerous growl above her head.

'I fancy you in the most shocking way, for a girl brought up in a convent. I've only to look at you and I go weak at the knees. Whenever you've touched me I've had to fight with myself for my honour. It really is humiliating of you to make me bare my soul in this way – but then you always were a rake.'

'And you, miss, had plenty of nerve from the very start.' With a sudden groan of a laugh he bent his head and crushed her lips in a long and thrilling kiss. 'Ynis, girl, bred from the magic of Welsh witches, I want you with all the shocking lust and all the tenderest passion my heart is capable of. To hell with Stella! She had my boyish love, and my adolescent body, but you, you green-eyed witch, you have the heart of me. Marry me – tomorrow? The banns have been called the required number of times. The house is waiting, the ghosts have gone.'

'I'll marry you, Gard.' Oh, they were lovely words to say, and as she said them all the ache left her heart. 'I'll love you as you have never been loved by your beautiful actress.'

'Beauty?' He held her face in his hand. 'You have more of that, my little love, than a dozen of her sort. You have beauty of spirit, and you have courage, girl, to take me on. Love won't tame my temper, nor will it bring back my right hand.'

'You think not?' Her smile was infinitely sweet in her love-bright eyes. 'What is this?' She placed her right hand against his heart. 'I give you mine, my darling Gard.'

He gazed down at her for a long moment, and now she could see into the darkness of his eyes and it seemed as if a beautiful little light burned inside them, making them the most wonderful eyes she had ever seen. 'If you are offering your hand, then I'll take it, Ynis. It can only lead me to heaven.'

'Oh, Gard, what a wonderful thing to say!'

They clung together, forged as one by a flame of love that burned out all the doubts, the pains, and the mistakes that two proud people can make when they fall in love. They were as one . . . now . . . tomorrow . . . until the very stars grew cold and died.

Lost together in that long, long kiss they didn't hear the door open, they didn't see a lean, light-haired man quirk a brow and quietly withdraw from the Regency room.

He knew, as heaven knew, that two lonely people had just found each other.

Mills & Boon Classics

The very best of Mills & Boon
romances, brought back for those
of you who missed reading them
when they were first published.

and in
February
we bring back the following four
great romantic titles

THE CASTLE IN THE TREES *by Rachel Lindsay*
The very name of the Castle in the Trees fascinated
Stephanie, and the reality was even more intriguing than
she had imagined. But there was mystery there too. Why
did Miguel and Carlos de Maroc hate each other? Stephanie
found out at last, but only at the cost of losing her heart.

ISLAND OF PEARLS *by Margaret Rome*
Many English girls go to Majorca for their holiday in the secret
hope of meeting romance. Hazel Brown went there and found
a husband. But she was not as romantically lucky as she
appeared to be — for Hazel's was a husband with a difference...

THE SHROUDED WEB *by Anne Mather*
For several very good reasons Justina wished to keep the news
of her husband's death from her frail, elderly aunt. Then she
heard of the Englishman Dominic Hallam, who was in hospital
suffering from amnesia, and the germ of an idea came into
her mind ...

DEVIL IN A SILVER ROOM *by Violet Winspear*
Margo Jones had once loved Michel, so when he died she
found herself going to look after his small son in the French
chateau of Satancourt. There Margo met Paul Cassilis, Michel's
inscrutable brother, to whom women were just playthings,
but in "Miss Jones" was to find one woman who was determined not to be.

If you have difficulty in obtaining any of these titles through
your local paperback retailer, write to:

Mills & Boon Reader Service
P.O. Box 236, Thornton Road, Croydon, Surrey, CR9 3RU.

The Mills & Boon Rose is the Rose of Romance

Every month there are ten new titles to choose from — ten new stories about people falling in love, people you want to read about, people in exciting, far away places. Choose Mills & Boon. It's your way of relaxing.

January's titles are:

BED OF GRASS *by Janet Dailey*
Judd Prescott had been the reason for Valerie leaving home. Now she was back, but Judd still didn't know what that reason had been . . .

WINTER WEDDING *by Betty Neels*
Professor Renier Jurres-Romeijn regarded Emily as a 'prim miss'. So it wasn't surprising that he so obviously preferred her lively sister Louise.

DANGEROUS DECEPTION *by Lilian Peake*
Anona Willis was engaged to the forceful Shane Brodie — but he had admitted that he had no staying power where women were concerned . . .

FEVER *by Charlotte Lamb*
The attraction between Sara Nichols and Nick Rawdon was immediate — but somehow Sara could never clear up the misunderstanding about her stepbrother Greg.

SWEET HARVEST *by Kerry Allyne*
Any thought of a reconciliation between herself and her husband soon vanished when Alix realised that Kirby had chosen her successor . . .

STAY THROUGH THE NIGHT *by Flora Kidd*
Virtually kidnapped aboard Burt Sharaton's yacht, Charlotte was told that if she didn't co-operate with him, he would ruin her father . . .

HELL OR HIGH WATER *by Anne Mather*
Jarret Manning was attractive, successful, experienced — and Helen Chase felt mingled antagonism and fear every time she met this disturbing man.

CANDLE IN THE WIND *by Sally Wentworth*
Shipwrecked, her memory lost, Sam had to believe her companion Mike Scott when he told her she was his wife . . .

WHITE FIRE *by Jan MacLean*
Rana had fallen wildly in love with Heath Markland, to the fury of her domineering mother. But perhaps she knew something about Heath that Rana didn't . . .

A STREAK OF GOLD *by Daphne Clair*
Eight years ago, Ric Burnett had cruelly told Glenna to get out of his life — but now they had met again . . .

If you have difficulty in obtaining any of these books from your local paperback retailer, write to:

Mills & Boon Reader Service
P.O. Box 236, Thornton Road, Croydon, Surrey, CR9 3RU